The Drifter

STAND-ALONE NOVEL

A Western Historical Adventure Book

by

Zachary McCrae

Disclaimer & Copyright

Table of Contents

Letter from Zachary McCrae

I'm a man who loves plain things; a cup of strong coffee in the morning, a good book at noon and his wife's embrace at night. I want to write stories that take you from the hand and show you what it meant to be someone who tried to make ends meet and find their own way in 19-century United States. I've been this someone for a long time in my life, always looking for my next gig after my parents' sudden death, always finding new friends but somehow not being able to stick with 'em. It's easy to find quantity in your life but what about quality?

At the age of 50, and after my baby boy, Jeb, and my sweet daughter, Janette, went away to study East, with my sweet wife, Mrs. Maryanne Mc Crae, we moved back to my home town and my dad's ranch close to the Rockies. After a series of health issues that have brought me even closer to our Lord, I've officially started writing those stories I always loved to read. I'm tending my land and animals now with the help of Maryanne, and I'm grateful for each day I get to walk on this world we call earth. As the saying goes, "Nature gave us all something to fall back on, and sooner or later we all land flat on it," so I want to take care of it just the way it has taken care of my dad and mom, and my cousins.

My adventure stories are my legacy to my children and to all of the readers that will honor me by following my work. God bless you and your families and our land! Thank you.

Stay safe but adventurous,

Zachary McCrae

Prologue

Natchez, Mississippi

January 1867

"Carve me a toy, Lee!"

"Me too!"

"No, it's my turn! Lee made you a horse last week!"

Lee Connor chuckled as he handed the wooden train car to one of the little girls clamoring around his workbench. "Here you go, Sally. The rest of you will have to wait until I'm not so busy. I can't stand around and carve toys all day. We've all got chores to do, so you better scoot!"

"Aw, Lee," the children grumbled. But slowly, following Sally with her new toy, they eased out of the decrepit barn, and headed home—the big, white, clapboard house everyone in town knew as the Mississippi Orphanage.

My thirty brothers and sisters. My family.

The little girls loved him, sure enough. As for the older ones—well, maybe one of these days. At nineteen, Lee considered himself nothing to turn a lady's head like the handsomer men in Natchez. Too tall and skinny, with hair the color of corn silk and a gap in his front teeth, he'd been told often enough his fetching smile and welcoming green eyes were his best features.

Come to think of it, the praise had come from the older-than-dirt washerwoman at the orphanage. The thought of having a real woman tell him he was handsome brought a blush to his tanned cheeks. At his age, he often thought of courting a woman, finding a wife—if he wasn't too embarrassed to kiss one.

"Hey, Lee." Twelve-year-old Frank, trudged into the barn, a worried frown on his gaunt face. "Where were you all day? Mr. Montgomery said I was to tell him when you got home. He wants to talk to you right quick. You think it's something bad?" Frank didn't quite wring his hands together, but Lee had seen him do it many times. Frank was the orphanage's worrier.

And we sure do have plenty of worries to go around. Not enough money, not enough food, not enough room and too many little mouths and bodies to take care of.

"Now, Frank," Lee answered, putting on a cheerful face although he felt far from pleasant himself. The day had begun long before dawn when he'd gone to help Mr. Baxter build a new stall for his prize mare. From there, with Mr. Montgomery's permission, Lee had walked four miles to another farm to help mend a farm fence.

The precious coins he'd earned would go for groceries and dry goods to keep the orphans fed another day. His feet and back ached like blazes, every muscle in his body screamed to sit down, but Sally'd been right there, wanting a toy. "Why would Mr. Montgomery want to talk about something bad?"

"He had an awful serious look on his face." Frank bit his lip. "Like it might be something bad an' he said, right away. The second I saw you."

Lee noticed how hollow the boy's pale cheeks looked and decided to make sure Frank got more of their meager supply of potatoes at supper. *Maybe I can trade one of the farmers nearby for some work for fresh cream. Frank should have more hearty food to build him up. All the little ones need heartier food.*

7

"You go tell him I'm home" Lee gave Frank a firm, reassuring pat on his thin shoulder, alarmed at the child's knobby bones beneath the threadbare pants. "I'm sure he just wants to know how much money I earned today. Mr. Montgomery's always looked out for us. Hasn't he always cared for us and done the right thing?"

"I—I reckon," Frank answered, not too certain.

"You know he has. Go tell him I'm home," Lee repeated. "I need to clean up here, so you tell him I'll be here in the barn. Unless he wants me to come up to his office."

Frank turned, glanced back once, and then hurried off.

Although Lee had told Frank there was nothing to worry about, he wasn't so certain himself. In the past few months, Mr. Montgomery had changed. Like Frank, Lee had noticed the director having an "awful serious look" on his face many times. *Wonder what's wrong?*

From as far back as he could remember, Lee knew he could trust and depend on Mr. Montgomery to look out for him. *He's my father. Maybe not a blood one, but my father anyway.* Wasn't it the director who helped him find outside work so he could help support the orphans? And wasn't it he who insisted Lee hold back some of his earnings for himself? "One day you'll want to strike out on your own, Lee, you keep some of that hard earned money for you."

Maybe he just wants to tell me about another job, Lee thought as he picked up his carving tools and stored them neatly on a shelf. *Or maybe he just wants to invite me to his office for a game of checkers.* As the oldest boy at the orphanage, Lee had privileges the other children didn't. He smiled, anticipating another pleasant evening with the man he thought of as his best friend. *Well, almost best friend-... after Thomas.*

Although lately, Lee thought as his hand mechanically swept up the wood shavings on the workbench, Mr. Montgomery didn't seem to have time for leisurely games of checkers or talking about the news he'd read in the papers. Lee had cherished the time with the older man, his knowledge passed on like a father to a son. No, lately, Mr. Montgomery seemed different, more tense and harried. *Was Frank right to be worried?*

Lee frowned, trying to figure out just when Mr. Montgomery had started to change from the kind, caring father he knew to a stricter taskmaster. *He used to be glad about me carving toys for the children, but lately...* "Lee? I must speak with you."

Startled, Lee turned to face the short, stout director of the orphanage. A scowl marked the man's florid face as he strutted into the barn, tugging down a worn gray vest over the wide girth of his stomach. *Been a long time since he's had a new suit of clothes. Wish I could buy him some.*

"Yes, Mr. Montgomery."

Lee bit his lip and hoped the director wasn't peeved to find him making toys. Mr. Montgomery didn't approve of the little ones playing these days. Life was real and earnest for the orphans. It took everyone pitching in to provide a garden for food and to keep the children in clean, hand-me-down clothes.

Some of the girls—barely eight and ten—helped with the washing and mending. Boys as young as five mucked out stalls and fed their meager assortment of cows, pigs, and chickens. Lee worked long, hard hours in the village to help add a few dollars a month to their coffers. Even though he worked hard, Lee figured the time spent making the children's lives happier was worthwhile too.

A simple wooden toy could bring a smile to the saddest little face. Not that this changed Mr. Montgomery would agree. *Not since when...* Lee couldn't figure out when he'd changed. *He used to give me toys he'd carved. Take me fishing and hunting. Taught me to play checkers.*

Lee brushed a lock of blond hair away from his face and mechanically swept wood chips from the front of his threadbare brown trousers—second or third hand-me-downs from the older boys who'd once lived here.

"Lee, I'm sorry to tell you this," Mr. Montgomery began in his hurried voice, the voice Lee thought of as the this-is-for-your-own-good one, right before he doled out a punishment. "But it's necessary for you to leave the home and set out on your own."

Leave? Although he knew that eventually he'd be asked to make his way in the world, Lee hadn't expected it this soon. Just a year ago, Mr. Montgomery had remarked how much he depended on Lee, on his working in town or at the neighboring ranches to earn money to keep the orphanage afloat. Hadn't the director often said how he hoped Lee would stay on for years? *When did he change? Why didn't I notice?*

Leave? The idea left Lee with the same sensation he'd had the night he accidentally fell down the well. Like a trapdoor had given way beneath him. He could only stand in stunned surprise.

"Yes, son." The word grated on Lee's mind, but he ground his teeth and stood tall. *How dare he call me son when he's turning me out?* But he wouldn't argue with Mr. Montgomery. What good would it do? If there was one thing being an orphan had taught Lee, it was to keep quiet and roll with what life sent your way.

"There was a yellow fever epidemic over in Raymond and the sheriff needs to send six boys here. And you know we are pressed for beds already."

Lee knew that for certain. He and two of the younger boys shared a room no bigger than a closet. "Even with what you earn working, we just don't have the funds to cover older boys staying on. You are nineteen. A man now. Old enough to make your own way in the world. I wouldn't ask if it wasn't necessary." For the first time in the conversation, the older man sounded sincere.

"I understand." *I don't! Why? You said you hoped I'd stay on and help you support the others! We've been short on beds before! It never used to matter.*

Lee's heart felt ripped in two, but he stood with dignity. Even though it crushed him inside to think of leaving the children he thought of as brothers and sisters, he wouldn't let Mr. Montgomery know that. *How am I going to tell the children?*

"The board of directors said to give you a month, that way you can make some plans and decide what you will do." Mr. Montgomery gave him a benevolent smile, as if he were personally handing him everything he needed to make his place in the world. "Perhaps you can find a permanent job or an apprenticeship. The preacher and his wife have generously given you a twenty-dollar gold piece to support yourself for a while, in thanks for the work you did on the sanctuary."

"Please tell them thank you," Lee said in a careful, calm voice. Inside, he raged. *What will I do? Where will I go?*

After Mr. Montgomery left the barn, Lee took time to sweep up the wood chips and clean the workbench he'd used the past three years. Even though most wood went to feed the fires in the stoves and fireplaces, Lee held back small pieces to create toys for the younger children—to make their lives brighter. Most of them had no family, barely enough to eat, and wore rags. Who would brighten their lives once he left? *It sure won't be Mr. Montgomery. Not this new one who sees only the number of bodies in the home and not their faces.*

Lee wasn't one to cry. He never had been. But suddenly, he felt tears burn in his green eyes. He was leaving his home— worse, he was leaving all his younger "brothers and sisters".

A month—it sure wasn't much time. but Lee had always yearned for adventures. He often told the younger boys' tales from the books he'd read when he had time for schooling. Adventure. Lee knew from reading that adventure took plans, but he'd never been really good at plans.

Now's the best time to learn, I guess.

Chapter One

"Lee! Lee Conner! You wait up, now!"

Lee stopped on the red clay farm road and turned to watch a short, wiry farmer with a halo of white hair hurry through a field of rye grass from his house. "Hi, Mr. Clemons. You need help with something today?"

The man stopped, wiped sweat from his face with a dirty, red kerchief and panted a little before he spoke. Even in January, the Mississippi weather could be warm enough to work up a sweat. Shaking his head, he gave Lee a gap-toothed smile, the three teeth he had left shining like pearl onions in his red gums. "No, nary a thing, but the wife and I heard you're moving on from the orphanage. Word around town says you be heading for Californee. That so?"

"Yes, sir." Even though it still hurt to acknowledge the fact he had to leave, Lee kept his feelings inside. Every fall the older couple let the orphans glean their corn fields or pick up windfalls in the apple orchard. He'd done odd jobs for Mr. Clemons and his wife through the years, bringing in welcome food and money for his orphanage family.

"We sure will miss you around here."

"Thank you kindly, sir."

"Reason I stopped you is—me and the missus want to help on your trip. So we're giving you Cletus. You're gonna need a horse to pull a wagon."

Cletus! Lee stared at the man incredulously. He had often ridden Cletus or used him to pull a wagon to take supplies to the orphanage. He and the Belgian got along well, and it had been one more thing he regretted about leaving—another wrench to his heart. "Why, Mr. Clemons, I can't take..."

"No, you listen to me, boy. I'm giving you the horse and Mr. Baxter's got a nice, light wagon you can take. Smaller than a Conestoga wagon, but since it's just you a-going it should hold your supplies fine."

A horse and a wagon? When Lee had first thought of heading to California, he'd written out a list of supplies he'd need. Although the *Emigrants' Guide to Oregon and California* written by Mr. Lansford W. Hastings recommended a horse and wagon or oxen, Lee knew he'd never be able to afford either.

A yoke of oxen cost around two hundred dollars and a good wagon at least a hundred. Most of his twenty-dollar gold piece would have to go for food that wouldn't spoil. Lee figured he'd just start walking until he could find a wagon train and join on with someone else, maybe as a hired hand. To his surprise, tears filled his green eyes and he had to blink. Maybe the old man understood.

"You'll find a lot of the neighbors gathered supplies for you, Lee. You've been a good neighbor all these years—always willing to help any of us in need. Why, when Mr. Baxter broke his leg and couldn't plow his wheat field, who came over at the break of dawn and did it before his own chores? You. When my wife was ailing and needed that medicine from the doc across the river, who was it rowed across and got it? We all love and care about you, boy. The wife wants me to tell you too—a lot of the women got stuff you'll need. Pots, skillets, an iron spider, blankets, and medicines. Tad Ewell at the Mercantile said he's fixing you up a couple of barrels of foodstuffs too. We been reading over that *Emigrant's Guide*, and you'll be outfitted as fine as we can make it."

"I don't know how to thank you," Lee blinked away tears; the words sounded husky around the knot in his throat. "You don't know what this means..."

"You're like a son to a lot of us around here, and we see how you help all those unfortunate mites at the orphanage. You're a good man, Lee, an' we aim to see you start off right."

He swallowed. "Thank you kindly, Sir."

"You're welcome. You best be on your way to wherever you was heading. I just saw you down here and wanted to make certain you stop by for Cletus afore you head off to Californee. Danged, if I was still a young blade, I'd go with you too. Take a crack at some of those gold fields!"

After he left Mr. Clemons, Lee hurried down the road and cut across at a path through a dense wood. He'd been on his way to his secret spot when he ran into the farmer. Only Lee knew which way to turn to keep his journey hidden. He'd never let any of the other children follow him here. Never told anyone of the secret place he'd found as an eight-year-old out exploring one day. No one except Thomas.

Just one more thing I owe you, *Thomas.*

Lee circled a small meadow and stepped through knee-high grass to an abandoned cabin. The cabin had fallen into disuse years ago and sunk into the cellar. A few spikes of rotting wood poked through the jungle of brush growing out of it. Blackberry thorns twisted and climbed over the crumbling brick ruins of a chimney. Even as an eight-year-old he'd never wanted to explore such a spooky place. But, behind the cabin, the owners had dug a small cellar.

To Lee's delight, he'd found a sturdy, hidden trap door, pulled away the persistent weeds of nutsedge, and discovered rickety wooden steps into an underground hidey-hole. When he'd first found the secret spot, nothing had been inside but a rusty pail and festoons of spiderwebs. Since then, he'd built a small shelf where he kept a jar of money he'd earned – a few pennies here and there from his wages.

15

Most of what he earned went to the orphans, but Lee knew a day would come when he'd be on his own. Without counting it, he knew it wouldn't amount to much. Every time there had been a need at the orphanage, he'd raided his cache to help.

On the shelf he also kept a wooden box he'd carved for his treasures—not so much really. A top he'd been given in a Christmas stocking. A nickel pierced through by a circus sharpshooter. The knife he'd used to carve his first toys, the tip nicked off now. He'd come for the one treasure he wanted to keep for his journey.

He rummaged through old marbles to pull out a *daguerreotype* he'd been given years ago by Mr. Montgomery. A different director than he'd been a few weeks ago when he'd told Lee he must leave. What had happened to the man who'd been more like a father? Lee sighed. He could remember so many happy times with the director.

The patient, fatherly way Mr. Montgomery had taught him and Thomas how to fish. So many lazy, warm, summer afternoons they'd sat on the bank of the Mississippi River talking about everything under the sun. The director never minded Lee's childish questions or seemed impatient. But now, he'd become so stern and hard. What had changed?

Lee stared at the daguerreotype in his hand, a picture from years ago. A visiting photographer had come to take a photo of the orphans and the home. Later, Lee learned it was sent to solicit funds for the orphanage. Lee stared at all the sad, frightened, or grim faces of the group of boys—forty-five at that time, lined up on the wide wooden steps of the big two-story building.

The gallery along the second floor filled with the girls in their white dresses and big hair bows. Some of them were so short they'd had to stand on wooden blocks, so their faces showed over the railing.

The boys were all dressed in Sunday best—blue serge suit jackets and pants with stiff white shirts. Lee had only ever worn that borrowed outfit once – for the photo. It was easy to pick out the director, Greg Montgomery, standing on the left with a gentle hand placed on the shoulder of Matt LeMont who had died of yellow fever a few months later. A smiling man, more friendly than he'd been in years. A happier time. *Why did you change, Mr. Montgomery? Did hard times sour you so much on life you gave up smiling?*

Lee found himself—skinny, gangly, the jacket sleeves inched up too far on his long gawky arms. Standing next to him was a tall, older boy with a crooked devil-may-care grin. Thomas.

I sure do miss you, Thomas.

Lee could never remember any life other than being an orphan. Even though Mr. Montgomery told him he'd been dropped at the home at age two by a distant cousin, Lee could only remember the Mississippi Orphanage. That was life. Most every day for those first four years of his life was the same as the one before. Until Thomas came.

Thomas hadn't been an orphan until he'd turned eight and his family died in a flood.

"Reason I didn't die," Thomas told the younger boys, "is 'cause I was playing hooky from school. Most everybody in the town died when the dam broke, but not ole' Thomas Stevenson. I'm too ornery to die."

Even though Lee didn't know if that was true, he found a true brother in Thomas. Thomas taught him basic skills like how to tie his shoes, to do chores, to hunt. Thomas never made fun of his clumsy attempts to learn how to whittle or the best way to make a slingshot. But when Lee turned eight, the terrible war between the states broke out.

"Soon as I can," Thomas promised one night after lights out, "I'm gonna join up an' fight for the Union."

"The Union?" Lee whispered, both thrilled that Thomas confided in him and scared to have him confess such a treasonous secret. Mississippi was a slave state and they'd been the second to secede from the Union. Mr. Montgomery said they were all Confederates now and took down the lithograph of Abraham Lincoln from the school room wall. "Our president is now Jefferson Davis," he had told the boys in a shaky voice. "Anyone who mentions the name of Abraham Lincoln is guilty of treason."

"Way I figure, them slaves want to be free just like us, Lee, boy." Thomas said as they whispered in the dark. "Old Abe Lincoln is a right just man. I figure if I can, I'm gonna help win this war."

Lee never told anyone about Thomas' betrayal. One morning he was just gone. Mr. Montgomery told everyone Thomas had gone to join up—to fight with "our daring men in gray." Lee didn't tell him any different. Through the years, he'd hoped for a letter or even Thomas himself to come back. He never did. Maybe he had died fighting for the Union.

Where did you go, Thomas?

Lee placed the daguerreotype in his pocket but left the marbles and the pierced nickel in the box. Maybe one of the other eight-year-olds in the orphanage would need a secret spot one day.

Chapter Two

February 1, 1867

Lee took a deep breath as he stood at the bare window of the only home he'd known for the past nineteen years. In the past few years, he'd earned a small bedroom of his own away from most of the younger boys. It was hardly more than a closet, but it held a creaky iron bedstead, with a trundle bed that pulled out from underneath for two of the younger boys, Danny and Jonny. A fine wooden table—Lee had carved it himself—-with an oil lamp. A wooden chair sat beside the table and a rag rug, braided by Mrs. Clemons, covered the worn, grayed planks of the floor.

Everything else Lee owned—which wasn't much—had been packed into his wagon.

Time to leave.

Even though he'd gotten up early to avoid having to say goodbye to the children, they thronged out the doors as he walked down the wooden steps, carrying a haversack he'd been given by Old Sam, the ancient caretaker. Old Sam had been someone's slave but had ended up at the orphanage during the war. Lee never knew the whole story, but he'd seen the brutal weals and scars from beatings on Sam's dark skinned back.

Watched the old man's dark brown eyes stare off with pain when he thought no one was looking. To Mr. Montgomery's credit, he asked no question, told no authorities. He'd given Old Sam a stall in the barn for a home and made sure the children treated him with respect. *Back then, Mr. Montgomery was more like the caring man I knew.*

Old Sam always made Lee glad Thomas had gone to fight for the Union. Even though he'd never dare tell anyone else. After the war, Lee tried to tell Old Sam about emancipation.

"I'll stay on here until the good Lord says my time's up," Sam had said after Lee read the newspapers about slaves being given their freedom in the north. "Ain't such a bad life here. Gets food and shelter, wood to heat my stove. Don't get beat or mistreated none."

Sam would not stand on the steps to see him off but gave Lee a gentle nod like a blessing from the side of the building. Lee made sure Sam could see him carrying the haversack. It was worn and old, but a gift from the old man's heart. He was going to miss Sam's benevolent dark face and his wisdom.

"Goodbye, Lee!" Six-year-old Sally cried openly as she hugged him around the middle. The other little girls each took a turn to hug him and wish him good-bye. Most of the little boys thought hugging was "sissy" but they all shook Lee's hand like "men" even though tears filled their eyes and spilled down their cheeks. Lee wished he'd thought of buying them candy. They so seldom had such a treat. But he'd stayed up until dawn most nights this month to carve them each a wooden toy to remember him.

Mr. Montgomery did not come outside to see him off. Lee hadn't expected the director, although he did see a curtain flick aside from the man's office. Lee had to blink away unexpected tears at this last betrayal. *I'm losing my father.*

Goodbye, Mr. Montgomery.

"Goodbye, everyone," he called to the tearful faces watching him leave.

His throat felt tight as he stepped into the wagon seat, released the brake, and snapped Cletus' harness. *Giddup!* The wheels creaked a little over the hard baked dirt of the front yard, pounded smooth by dozens of bare feet. Lee blinked hard as he turned into the road past the two brick gate posts of the orphanage.

Goodbye, Mississippi Orphanage.

"Well, Cletus, I reckon we're bound for California."

Lee drove past all his neighbors, silently wishing them well in the early dawn hours. The sun rose in the east behind him, warming him until he had to pull off the plaid flannel shirt he'd worn in the chill predawn air.

He made a brief stop in the village, where Mrs. Baxter ran out with a freshly baked loaf of bread and a small jar of strawberry preserves. Other neighbors waved from windows or doorways, wishing him well. A small stirring of excitement warmed Lee's heart.

I'm on the road to adventure! Even though he felt the loss of the children he'd left behind, he knew it was time to think about the journey ahead. There could be no turning back. In front of him he faced over seven hundred miles of travel until he could reach Independence, Missouri to meet a wagon train. *I hope.* Despite his anticipation, Lee also felt a weight of apprehension about going all those miles. It was February. At the best pace he could set, he wouldn't reach Missouri until April. Would he find a wagon train ready to set out for California? Folks said most trains began about then to reach California before snow fell in the mountains.

He'd traveled about five miles past the village when he heard a rustle in the wagon bed behind him.

Mice? Had something gotten into his barrels of flour and beans? Although he'd eaten a lot of food with vermin in his years at the orphanage, Lee didn't like the idea of mice eating his newly purchased supplies. If there were mice in the barrels, he'd set them out right here and now. Those barrels of food needed to last for a while.

"Whoa, Cletus!" Lee jerked on the reins, put on the brake, and went around to pull apart the canvas cover of the wagon bed. Before he could climb into the back, a familiar towheaded face peered over the barrel of beans. "Hi, Lee!"

"Danny! What are you doing here?"

Seven-year-old Danny had been most persistent in hearing tales of Lee's upcoming adventures. He wanted to know it all—question after question until even Lee's patience wore thin, and then "just one more question" at night from the trundle bed.

"I want to come with you on your adventures."

Lee stared at the little boy, annoyed and aggravated. Already five miles down the road and now he'd have to retrace those steps to take him back to the orphanage. He'd lose most of the day turning back. The weight of those seven hundred miles before him pressed down on his mind like an andiron. "Danny, you can't come with me! What'll Mr. Montgomery say?"

"He don't care. He's got too many kids now. I heard him tell the washerwoman he wished some of us would get lost or something. He's got all those new boys coming from the epidemic. He won't miss me."

"He says things like that but he's still in charge of you." Lee pulled off his wide-brimmed hat and slapped it against the knee of his new blue trousers. The first pair of new pants he'd had in years. "Darn it—now I've got to take you back and lose a day's travel."

Surely, once he'd gone back to the orphanage it would be time to camp for the night. He'd have to go through all the goodbyes again. The very idea turned his stomach and clenched his heart. *I can't!*

"Please, Lee, don't take me back." Danny's blue eyes widened in alarm, the freckles dark as nutmeg over his chalky face. "You know what'll happen if you take me back. I'll get a switching for running off."

Lee stopped, remembering Mr. Montgomery's punishment for misdeeds. He'd had plenty of switchings from the director's firm, unrelenting hands too. "I'm sorry about that, Danny, but it's too dangerous to take you with me. I'm not certain what I'll find. I've got to get to Missouri, to meet up with a wagon train if I can find one. Then there's a lot of harsh land between here and California. A lot of danger."

"You're going."

"I'm a man," Lee said although he felt about as young as Danny just then. How did a man know what was right or wrong? "You're just a little boy. Anything could happen to you."

"Please, Lee. Can't you write Mr. Montgomery a letter or something and tell him you decided to adopt me? That way I can go along with you. You don't want me to live there until I'm old like you, do you? Ain't nobody ever wants me when people come looking. Not even as a farm hand. Nobody's gonna adopt me."

Lee had to admit, anyone who came hoping to adopt an orphan usually passed Danny over. He'd been dropped at the orphanage at three with something wrong with his leg. Although he could walk fine, one leg twisted sideways, and it made him slower than normal. Farm chores took him longer than the other boys and despite Mr. Montgomery's orders that he be left alone to work at his own pace, some of the older boys teased him mercilessly.

What kind of life would he have? Living at the orphanage until he got turned out? How could he make a living for himself? Unlike Lee, who could earn a decent living doing chores or picking up carpentry work, Danny had no skills to fall back on.

"Please? I brought along my clothes," Danny held up a ragged string bag, "got some shirts an' a couple pairs of britches. Jonny even give me his new handkychef."

"Handkerchief," Lee corrected automatically but his throat closed tight at the sight of Danny's pathetic bag of hand-me-downs.

"I guess you ain't got much of a future at the orphanage." Lee said, hoping he was making the right decision. Now that he'd pointed himself west, headed toward California, Lee didn't want to turn back. It might be a sorry excuse to keep traveling on, but Lee figured it was honest. "All right, you can travel along with me." Lee figured he'd been taking care of the little boys at the orphanage for years anyway. Having Danny along might be nice too, give him someone to talk to beside Cletus. Lee wouldn't admit it to anyone else, but those few miles since the village sure felt lonesome without a bunch of chattering voices. "But I'm like your Pa or big brother. You got to do what I say, you hear? And I can use a switch same as Mr. Montgomery."

"Sure," Danny agreed with a cheeky grin, as if he knew Lee would never punish him. "Can I ride up front with you now?"

"I reckon. Let's get back on the road." What he would say to Mr. Montgomery, he didn't know, but Lee planned to write to him from the next town and send a letter. Like Danny said, the director would probably be glad to have one less mouth to feed. Even though he never used to be like that.

They managed another six miles before Lee thought it best to stop and camp. He felt good about their distance—a little over eleven miles if he figured it right. Not bad for his first time on the road. Near as he could figure, it would take about two months to travel the distance to Missouri.

They were off to a good start. Cletus showed signs of weariness and Lee's back side needed to get up and stretch. Although Danny kept up his chatter most of the time, the last couple of miles had him nodding off on the hard wagon seat.

"Reckon we should find a camp spot for the night," Lee said, "fix us some supper and feed Cletus. Help me look for a nice spot."

"There's a good place." Danny pointed to a shady area up ahead.

About half a mile down the road, they saw a small stream, a few trees nearby and level ground to set the wagon. Lee jumped out of the wagon seat and began to unhitch the horse. Cletus strained to get near the water, so he let Danny take the harness and lead the horse to the stream. "Looks like a storm might be brewing in the east."

A dark ominous cloud rolled across the evening sky. Lee figured they might need shelter for a while. He'd placed the wagon near the trees, but not too close in case of lightning. Taking an India rubber poncho tent from the wagon, he stretched it from the wagon bed and pegged it into the ground to make a lean-to. After scouting around for loose kindling, Lee dug a pit and built a small campfire beneath the lean-to. Kind of smoky, but the rain wouldn't put out their warmth.

When Danny brought Cletus back, Lee tied him to a picket rope near the side of the wagon. He'd have to hope the trees gave him some shelter from the rain. "Too bad we didn't come across an abandoned cabin," Lee joked, "then Cletus and us could have camped in style."

Thunder rolled, but Cletus, cropping fresh grass near the wagon, appeared not to care. He flicked a dusty ear at the sound, glanced at the sky and bent to crop another bite between his yellow teeth. "He might be glad to have it rain on him," Danny decided as he crawled under the lean-to and sat on a pallet of blankets Lee had fixed for his bed. "It's kind of a hot day, and he must get tired being in a fur coat."

Lee laughed. "You could be right."

Lightning flickered in the distance the whole time Lee cut a slab of bacon and fried it in the iron skillet. He made a pot of coffee, thankful again for Mr. Ewell at the general store who had fixed enough supplies to get him as far as Missouri. Most wagon trains set out from there and Lee hoped he could buy more supplies. If not for his neighbors in Natchez, he'd have been ill-prepared to supply his trip. He had to figure God had a hand in it somehow and the Lord had provided as Old Sam always said.

As the first gentle pattering of rain came, he and Danny were nice and dry on waterproof gum blankets and bed rolls under the tent. The fire was a bit smoky in their tiny bedroom, but the bacon fried up hot and crisp along with hoe cakes and coffee to wash it down. A cool breeze, scented with rain, freshened the air.

"You cook good," Danny mumbled with his mouth full. Bacon grease smeared his face and hoe cake crumbs dotted the front of his blue shirt. The little boy sat on his pallet and gave a sleepy yawn.

"Reckon I oughta," Lee took another drink of coffee and leaned back against the wagon bed. A moderate rain kept up another half hour until Danny announced, "Hey, Lee, what do we do for an outhouse out here? I gotta..."

Lee chuckled.

"Got the whole outdoors for an outhouse. Go behind a tree or something like you're in the woods."

"I'll get all wet."

Danny crinkled his nose in disgust and looked out at the rain. He waited a few more minutes, sighed and ducked under the tent. He walked behind the wagon, near a tree.

Later, Lee could never tell exactly what happened.

An enormous *CRACK!* split the air. A jagged bolt of lightning crackled and sizzled like a 4th of July firecracker. It lanced through the rain and cleaved the tree behind the wagon in two. The trunk split and fell with a loud thud on the saturated ground, shooting up a geyser of mud. Cletus jerked and whinnied on the picket rope but didn't appear to be harmed. *But what about...*

Trembling, Lee tossed the tin mug from his hand and ducked under the tent.

Danny!

Chapter Three

"Danny!"

Only silence except for the rumbling rolls of thunder and frequent crackles of lightning. *Oh, Danny, Danny... I should have taken you home!* Lee started for the split tree when Danny stumbled from the back of the wagon, eyes wide as gopher holes, his mouth opening and closing like a fish tossed up on the shore.

"Danny, are you hurt?"

The boy stared at him terrified, opening and closing his mouth.

"Are you hurt?"

Danny's words screamed out shrill and loud. "I can't hear you, Lee! I see your mouth moving but I can't hear you!"

Lee didn't know what to do. Had he brought Danny out here only to have him lose his hearing in a freak accident? The sound of the lightning must have damaged his ears somehow. Suddenly, Lee wished they were both still safe in the decrepit barn carving toys.

The little boy's blue eyes streamed tears. His sobs came loud and gut-wrenching.

Thinking of the many times Thomas had helped him through trouble, Lee took a deep breath. *Now it's my turn to be Thomas.*

Turning Danny to face him, Lee yelled, "It must have been the noise of the lightning! You'll be okay in a few days."

"I can't hear!" Danny screamed. "My ears got blowed off! I can't hear!"

Lee shook the boy until Danny stared back, his freckled, tear-streaked face etched with desperation. "Look at me, Danny. You will be all right. I've heard tell of men who lost their hearing being near dynamite on the railroad. It came back in a few days. I'm sure yours will too." He took Danny's hands and placed them over his ears so the boy could feel them still attached to his head.

"H-honest?" Danny choked out the word in a more normal voice, touching his ears for assurance.

"I'm certain," Lee lied. Even though he wasn't at all.

Danny was so upset Lee decided to make a potion for his ears. Maybe if Danny thought there was medicine he might get better. Lee had seen it work many times before when one of the orphans was ill. Doc Tremont even chuckled about how his "special syrup" had cured many an illness. Lee knew for a fact that the "special syrup" was blackberry juice and a spoonful of cod liver oil.

The storm ebbed away into the distance. A few final patters of rain came from the trees and Cletus settled back down on his picket rope. The tree struck by lightning smoldered but did not catch fire or appear to be a danger to the wagon.

"I've got medicine for ears," Lee shouted while Danny watched his lips. "I'm going to put some in yours."

Lee climbed inside the wagon and opened a small box of medicine and herbs Mrs. Baxter had given him. She'd even written down some receipts for various ailments. Lee's eyes roved through the entries in her even, Palmer script until he found one for "earache." It used mustard oil, warmed, and dropped into the ear.

He had no idea if it would help, but if Danny thought so, it might do the job. Lee got a spoon and poured a splash of mustard oil in the spoon. He held the spoon over the campfire and let it warm for a minute or two. Motioning for Danny to lie down on his pallet, Lee carefully dropped the mustard oil in one ear at a time.

"This will help you," Lee shouted so Danny could see his lips move. "It'll fix you right up."

Danny sniffled but otherwise didn't complain. When Lee motioned him to go ahead and get into bed, the little boy crawled beneath the warm woolen blanket. Lee woke every so often during the night, listening to Danny crying in his sleep. *What am I going to do?* He questioned the idea of taking Danny back to the orphanage. But did he really want to turn around and travel eleven miles back to the place where he'd started? *No!* What good would it do anyway? Unable to hear, Danny would have an even harder time finding someone to love him. *It's my fault*, Lee decided as dawn crested in the East. *Guess Danny is my responsibility now.*

The next morning, Danny's hearing still hadn't come back. With more assurance than he felt, Lee mixed up more mustard oil and dropped it in Danny's ears. They made breakfast, broke camp, and were soon on the way. They'd traveled about an hour when Danny tugged at Lee's arm and pointed to a maple tree up ahead.

"Hey," Lee stared at the brown lump tied to a tree, blinked to make sure he wasn't dreaming, and stared again. Horns? "It looks like an ox."

"Whoa, Cletus."

The ox looked at them with weary, apathetic eyes, as if he'd given up on life. Lee's heart went out to the creature. He'd seen plenty of orphans with just that look.

"He looks tired out and parched," he said as he got down to examine the animal closer. Then realizing Danny couldn't hear him, he turned the boy's face so he could read his lips. "He needs food and water."

Danny nodded, ran to grab the feed bucket, and scooped out some grain from a barrel. He ran to place it before the ox. The animal sniffed in interest. He unfolded his short legs, trembling a little at the activity, stood, and began to nibble the grain.

"Water," Danny shouted.

Lee took another bucket and scooped out a portion from their water barrel. The animal slurped as if he hadn't had a drink in days. "He's going to need more watering, maybe some rest," Lee said mostly to himself. Danny stood near the ox, watching with eager eyes as the animal's brown eyes gazed up at him unafraid. Lee looked around at their surroundings.

"Wonder who tied him to a tree and why?" Lee muttered more to himself than Danny. "What kind of a cruel person would do such a thing?"

A short distance away, he noticed a small watering hole and figured they'd best just make camp now. He chafed at the delay, only a few miles' travel today, but it would be cruel to abandon the animal. After he'd motioned to Danny what he intended to do, Lee drove the wagon near the water. Danny led the ox and tied him with a picket rope so he could drink. If they let it rest, it might be an asset to them on the trail—or he could sell it in Missouri for supplies. Once again God had provided.

"We'll rest here a few days." Lee turned Danny so the boy could understand. "So we can take him with us."

"What's his name?" Danny shouted, still uncertain how loud his voice sounded.

"You can name him if you want to."

Danny looked at the animal, walked around him, and bit the corner of his lip. "How about Charlie?" Danny yelled. "He looks like a Charlie. Hi, Charlie, you want to go to California with us?"

Lee grinned, happy to see Danny acting more like himself. Maybe God had sent Charlie along for more than one reason.

***

An agonizing month later, Lee began to wonder how far it was until they'd meet up with another wagon. They hadn't seen anyone for days except for a grizzled old man in a rundown cabin who had let them camp out in his falling-down barn for the night. Lee figured they had crossed the Missouri line at some point but there was no way of knowing for sure.

"There's a town some forty miles west," the old man said, spitting a wad of brown, chewed tobacco at Lee's feet, "but I ain't been there in years."

Even with all the supplies Mr. Ewell had given them, Lee knew they'd run out of flour and beans before too long. Feeding Danny meant having meals for two instead of one. Having to give the ox some of the extra grain they'd brought along for Cletus worried him too. What if they came to places where the animals couldn't graze at night? Lee knew from reading the *Emigrant's Guide* that the California Trail could lead through some mighty stark land without grass for grazing. So far, by staying as close to the Mississippi River as possible, they'd done okay with the animals' food and water.

Lee tried to keep up his spirits for Danny, but he couldn't deny he'd begun to doubt this adventure. Maybe he should have stayed in Natchez, gotten a job at the Livery, or tried for an apprenticeship with Old Man Miller who ran a fine gunsmith shop. *Thomas, what would you have done?* Even though everyone said California was the land of opportunity, did that make it right for Lee?

"When you think we'll get to the other wagons, Lee?" Danny had asked the night before. Although his hearing hadn't come all the way back yet, each day Danny was able to hear better. Two nights before, he'd heard the lonesome howl of a wolf and been startled out of sleep. Lee could only pray the boy would recover all the way.

"Soon, I hope," Lee raised his voice so Danny could hear, glad when the boy nodded his understanding of the words.

The wagon creaked along a dirt packed road in the middle of nowhere for another lonely week. Even Danny finally ran out of things to chatter about as the wagon creaked along behind Cletus' plodding, surefooted steps. Some days, Lee let the ox pull the wagon and Cletus ambled along tied behind. He got weary of the jolts and jars of the wagon hitting ruts or creaking over rocks.

Lee began to wonder if they had missed a turn off somewhere and were headed for the end of the world. He knew in his mind the world was round, but out here with just trees and an endless dirt packed trail—sometimes lost in the tall grass—he began to wonder if he and Danny were the last two people left on the earth. They saw plenty of rabbits, gophers, prairie dogs and even a few lone antelopes, but no people. At the end of another endless, sun beating down day, weary to the point of nodding off on the hard wooden wagon seat, Lee's eyes stared at a strange blob of white canvas billowing in the distance.

Could it be?

Is it—

"It's a wagon!" Danny shouted. "A covered wagon like us!"

Even Cletus seemed to catch the excitement and stepped higher as they crossed the grassy road toward the other wagon. A wagon settled for the night by a stream, beneath a small stand of willows. A glowing campfire sent out sparks of welcome. Even though Lee hadn't felt hungry, the scent of frying beef and rich coffee caused his stomach to rumble. *Thank you again, God.*

As they rode closer, a man and a woman stood from logs they'd pulled near the campfire. The man was tall and lean with a rich dark face like Old Sam's. The woman was short and a bit slumped, shaped like an overripe pear, and a worried look flickered across her warm brown face.

"Welcome," the man called out, but kept his hand on a revolver tucked in the waistband of a pair of loose, linen pants. Although the woman gave them a timid smile, she kneaded her fingers nervously in the folds of a bright yellow apron over a dark red dress. Fear narrowed her eyes.

"Howdy." Lee pulled up the wagon, tugged Cletus to a halt and pushed on the brake. He tipped his hat at the couple, wondering whether they were slave or free. No matter what changes the War had brought, people were slow to change, and some blacks were still treated like slaves. He understood their hesitancy and hoped to make them feel at ease. "I'm Lee Connors and this is my... my brother, Danny. We sure are mighty glad to meet up with you folks," Lee hurried on, hoping the couple would know he meant them no harm. The woman kept looking around in fear as if expecting the worst. "We thought we were the last folks left in the world! It got mighty lonely the last few miles."

The man must have sensed there was no danger. His hand left the top of the revolver, and he stepped forward to take Lee's outstretched hand. "James Richards and this here's my wife, Erica."

"Pleased to meet you, Mr. Richards. Ma'am." Lee grinned. Mississippi might have been a slave state before the war, but Mr. Montgomery had always made sure they were respectful to their elders. If Old Sam hadn't insisted on being called, "Old Sam," the director would have had them call him Mr. Sam. *Come to think of it, Mr. Montgomery never did seem like a true Mississippian about slavery. Heard him whisper once how it was an "abhorrent practice."*

The woman looked at Danny and spoke for the first time in a soft, melodious voice. "Would you and the little one like to join us for supper? Not much, but we can share what we have."

"Yes!" Danny shouted for both and leapt off the wagon seat. "I'm hungry enough to eat a bear!"

"Ain't got no bear," James said with a chuckle, "but a mighty tasty roast of beef we brought from home in Ohio."

Lee smiled as he climbed stiff-legged from the hard wagon seat. "As soon as I tend to my animals, we'd be pleased to join you. But only if you let us contribute to the meal too. I fried up some hoe cakes for lunch and we got maple syrup we'd be pleased to share."

Mrs. Richards clapped her hands in delight. "Maple syrup? Haven't had a sweet in a month of Sundays. We'll have us a feast!"

Just coming across another wagon, headed for the same adventures he faced, made Lee feel at peace for the first time since he'd turned the wagon out between the brick posts of the orphanage. *We aren't alone!* A new surge of hope rose in his heart.

We're going to make it! California, here we come!

Chapter Four

Somewhere Past Missouri

March or April 1867

Now. Tonight.

Nancy Fitzgerald lay fully clothed on a cot in the wagon, holding her breath and listening. Her cornflower blue eyes stared at the canvas wagon cover overhead. The mass of brown curls that usually cascaded to her waist, she'd pulled tight into a long braid. One less problem to worry about when she made her escape. She clenched her delicate hands together, almost in prayer. *Can I run away this time?*

From under the wagon bed came the loud, rumbling breathing of Uncle Brad, sleeping in a drunken stupor. As usual.

If I can just get away!

She had planned it so many times before. Once, she'd even managed to pack a satchel and buy a ticket for the afternoon stage out of Little Rock. Her mistake had been in not hiding Mr. Morgan's letters or taking them with her.

Of course, Uncle Brad had found them and come after her. He'd ripped the ticket in half, taken her home, and used his leather belt to beat her into submission. He'd never let her leave the farm alone again—not even to join her friends for a picnic social. *Not that I had many friends—just one, really. Susie.*

Nancy had to figure that God—if He ever noticed folks like her—had given her this second chance. Uncle Brad had come home one afternoon, announcing that he'd sold the Arkansas farm and they were moving to California! He had a friend who had made a fortune during the gold rush and urged Uncle to come.

If there was one thing Uncle was good at besides being an ornery drunkard, it was greedy. Why labor on a farm, doing the back-breaking job of making a living, when there was gold dust in California just washing out of the streams?

Nancy had no illusions about her role in this new scheme. As always, she would be expected to cook, wash, clean and do chores so that Uncle could drink, curse, and use his leather belt if she moved too slowly.

Nancy's breathing came in short, nervous bursts and her heart thundered beneath the chest of her second-best blue dress. *I've got to get away.*

In the satchel under the cot was one letter that spelled her freedom. After Uncle had discovered the others and torn them to shreds, Nancy found one she had hidden. She'd waited until the light of a full moon to sew the precious scrap of paper into the sawdust inside her pin cushion. Although Nancy was scared to face the unknown, it was a risk she'd have to take. Surely, Mr. Morgan, who sounded like a fine gentleman in his letters, would be a good husband. Better than living with Uncle—being almost a slave to him since Mama died.

It was the thought of Mama that gave Nancy the courage to ease off the cot. Barefoot, her toe hit the edge of a tin bucket. The clatter seemed to go on forever as it banged into a barrel of cornmeal. *No! No! Don't wake up!*

Uncle's breathing sputtered, like a horse breathing through its nose, then settled back. He coughed. She stood stiff as a washboard, hardly daring to breathe, until it sounded as if he'd gone back to sleep.

Waiting to be sure, Nancy went over her plans again. *I'll take Beauty. She's my horse, after all. Mama bought her for me.* And Beauty couldn't pull Uncle's wagon all the way to California anyway. At some point, Uncle would sell Beauty and there'd be nothing she could say. Nancy also had a few coins she'd managed to hold back from the grocery money Uncle doled out like a miser. It had been hard. She'd also taken a few greenbacks from the stash in Uncle's strongbox. Maybe he'd forget how much he had.

If I can just find a wagon train, maybe there'll be a nice family who needs a nursemaid or a woman to help. If not, I'll walk. Every single step of the way. I will get there.

Although she had no idea how she'd get to Mr. Morgan. *Maybe I'm hoping for too much?*

Nancy had no fancies about Mr. Morgan. No dreamy-eyed imaginings as her friend, Susie, did about falling in love. *If he's kind and peaceable, if he can build me a sweet little house with white pillars on the porch, then we'll be fine. If he's not like Uncle, I don't care if I'm not madly in love with him.* Nancy wasn't sure she'd know true love if it came up and hit her over the head. Except for mama, love had been in short supply in her life.

Now! Nancy crept forward on tip-toe, carrying her high button shoes, and eased down from the wagon bed. She walked across the dewy grass to Beauty.

"Where are you going?" Uncle rasped out, crawling from beneath the wagon.

She gasped. *No, no, no!*

"Where are you going, girl?" He scratched the chest of his unwashed long johns.

"I'm l-leaving."

"Leaving? To where?"

Nancy dared not mention Mr. Morgan. Not after the beating she'd suffered when Uncle found his letters before. "I'm going anywhere! Away from you. I ha-hate you. You killed Mama!" It wasn't how she'd meant to face him, but Nancy couldn't help the outburst.

"You are going nowhere, you ungrateful wench." He came toward her, reeking of sweat, stale whiskey, and unwashed clothing.

With a sickening dread, Nancy watched him yank off his thick leather belt, double it, and pull her close enough to hit. It did no good to resist as he began to beat her across the back and shoulders. Even though it stung through the thin fabric of her dress, she refused to cry, to let him know he'd hurt her. Nancy ground her teeth; hot tears burnt in her eyes, but she blinked them back.

He kept hitting her, yelling unspeakable things about her— words Nancy had heard but didn't quite understand. It didn't matter that she didn't know everything he meant. The words cut deeper than the beating.

Finally, he lost steam and breathing hard, almost panting, he stopped. "Get back in the wagon. We are going to California and you're going with me. You are worthless— cooking and cleaning, that's all you're good for!"

Nancy climbed back into the wagon and then gave way to silent sobbing, pounding her hands on the pillow. She would never get away from him. Never. It was hopeless.

***

In the morning, she got up and started to prepare breakfast, stiff and sore from the beating the night before. Carrying a pail of water from a nearby stream set her shoulders to screaming in pain. She dare not complain. Nancy quietly went about her chores, starting a fire, brewing coffee, frying bacon and cornbread.

Uncle glowered at her as he brooded over his tin mug of coffee. She hated every inch of him from the balding top of his head to the tips of his worn, black boots. Boots she was expected to polish for the times he went off to the saloon in Little Rock to meet his cronies. "Sit down, girl, we've got to talk."

Nancy obeyed. Even though she'd fixed herself a tin plate of food, her throat closed too tight to eat a morsel. She set the plate on her lap and sat on a stump. Since she'd lost her mama at twelve, Uncle was her guardian, the dispenser of justice. His twisted sense of right and wrong ruled her life.

Even as a child, with Mama to take up for her, Uncle had meted out punishments as he saw fit. It had done no good to run crying to Mama. "I'm sorry sweetie, but he is like a father to you, and we are living with him." Mama might have despised her brother's treatment of Nancy, but she'd been held prisoner too by the need to have a home. "In these times, Nancy," Mama often said, "there's no other choice for a woman without a husband. Since your papa died before you were born, we need to be grateful my brother took us in. He's our provider and no matter what we think of him, we must do as he says."

"You're a whore." Uncle's words were like a fist to the stomach.

Nancy gasped, eyes wide as the tin plate tipped forward and spilled from her lap. Hardly aware that the bacon draped across her bare feet, she wanted to speak but was too shocked.

How could he call me such a wicked name? Nancy had heard the word whispered in town. In some part of her mind, she knew it was a woman who did "bad" things with a man, although she had no idea what those bad things could be. It wasn't something talked about in polite company. Maybe it was one of those things girls whispered about among themselves, but she'd never known enough girls to be sure.

She had never been with a man, never even dared speak to one in town, although several had taken the liberties of smiling when she did her shopping. Had that been wrong or wicked to return a smile? Or... a wave of guilt assailed her. Once, after Sunday School, Mr. Paul Durant had asked, in a timid, stuttering voice, if he could escort her to the church social. Even though Nancy refused, terrified Uncle would find out and beat her for being so forward as to encourage his attentions, she worried for days. Had she led Mr. Durant on?

"I—I'm not," she managed to whisper, but in her mind she worried. Surely Uncle was older and would know such things. Guilt washed over her, and Nancy's stomach churned. Is *it* *true?*

"You've thrown yourself at a man!" Uncle hollered with a leering sneer on his ruddy face, his blood shot eyes glaring at her. "You're worse than a soiled dove, you're a..."

Nancy had never heard the vile word he shouted, much less understood what it meant. But in her heart, she knew it meant something wrong, dreadfully wicked. Had writing to Mr. Morgan turned her into a tainted woman? Was it wrong? It hadn't felt wrong. But perhaps it was—maybe she *had* thrown herself at a man. If only Mama was still alive and could advise her!

"You are lower than dung and I'm done with you."

He stood up and threw the tin cup at her bare feet. Coffee splashed over her toes and for the first time Nancy noticed the spilled plate of food, the bacon and coffee burning against her skin. Trembling, she reached down and wiped her feet with a linen towel. Uncle stalked to the wagon and began to rummage through it.

Nancy couldn't move. She watched as Uncle yanked out a worn satchel of his clothes. Before her incredulous eyes he rolled up a bedroll, saddled one of the horses and tossed his belongings across it as if preparing for a journey. He climbed into the back of the wagon and came out with the small, black strongbox where he'd packed their worldly wealth—all the money he had in the world.

He'll know I stole money!

Nancy held her breath, her face growing pale. He would give her the worst whipping she'd ever had. Bile rose in her mouth. She fought to keep from heaving at the dread she felt. To her shock, he didn't appear to notice her theft. He took care to count out most of the greenbacks and coins. Then he tossed the strongbox and a meager amount of coins at her feet.

"Here, you whore! Your mother made me promise I'd give you a dowry. There it is. Take the wagon and your horse. No one can say I didn't honor your mother's request. I'm going on to California and make my fortune. I'm through with you."

"But, what... what am I supposed to do? Where will I go?"

"You'll find a man. Any man, most likely." He glared at her with disgust from his rheumy eyes. "That's all you need is a man to see you through. You're wicked and vile. A woman who'd write such letters to a man she's never met. Throwing yourself at a man like a whore."

Nancy sucked in a ragged breath. Writing to Mr. Morgan didn't feel wrong. Had it been? *Am I wicked? A soiled dove? What does that mean anyway?*

Uncle came close to her face and spit. "I wash my hands of you."

To her fear, he mounted his loaded horse, kicked his spurs into the horse's sides and rode away. He never looked back. Nancy stood there, too stunned to wipe the slimy spittle off her face, and watched him ride down the trail. It was only when the acrid scent of burning bacon from the skillet on the campfire met her nose that she came to her senses. *I'm alone.*

Even though she'd planned to run away last night, being abandoned on the trail suddenly felt like the scariest thing in the world.

I'm alone!

ZACHARY MCCRAE

Chapter Five

Independence, Missouri

April 1867

"I sure never thought we'd make it here," Lee said to Danny as the ox pulled their wagon through the teeming city street. After so many weeks of staring at nothing but trees, barren land and sun-squinting horizons, the hustle and bustle of Independence assaulted their eyes. Stores and shops of every variety lined the crowded streets, board sidewalks swarmed with men, women and children hurrying to and fro. Dust rose from all the commotion in the wide, dirt-packed street to choke Lee's breath and water their eyes.

"It hurts my ears," Danny shouted to be heard over all the noise. Lee agreed. After weeks of listening to the creak of the wagon wheels, the steady clops of Cletus or the ox, and the wind whistling through the trees at night, city noises were harsh and beat the ears like a dozen people banging spoons on tin pans.

Horses whinnied, cattle and oxen lowed, people shouted or hollered, voices chattered in so many different accents it was hard to take it all in. Dozens of wagons lined the streets with worldly goods tied or roped to the sides. One wagon, bigger than any Lee had seen so far, had a cage with some mighty angry chickens squawking their disapproval of the whole trip. Feathers flew. Two little girls peered from one canvas cover; eyes big in their sunburnt faces. A woman snapped. A dog barked from beneath another wagon then went back to gnawing on a bone. Hammering, creaking, sounds they couldn't identify shattered the morning. Men cursed and others laughed.

"Sure does," Lee hollered back. "My nose too!"

If Lee had to describe the scents, he'd have been hard pressed. There was the ever-present odor of manure and dung, horse hide, unwashed bodies, ladies' scent, sunbaked wood, mildew and a hundred other nose-pinching smells. A somewhat pleasant scent of frying eggs and coffee came from one tidy house until the odd, sickening sweet odor of a saloon door opening overpowered it.

Danny crinkled his nose in agreement. "It sure did take a long time to get here. Are we in California now?"

Lee chuckled. "Far from it—we've got miles to go. This is just where we meet up with a wagon train so we can all travel together. I guess it's another four or five months until we hit California." *And where will we go when we get there?* Again, fear came rushing back. Fearful thoughts that had followed him every mile of the trail from Natchez. He'd have to find a way to make a living for himself and Danny. Build a cabin. Start crops. Or would it be better to find a town and work for someone to build up a grubstake? *What would Thomas do? Sure wish you were here to help me.*

"Why?"

"Why, what?"

"Why do we have to travel with other wagons?" Danny repeated. "We got the Richards."

Danny had been spending most of his time with the Richards since they'd met up on the trail that fortunate night. They seemed to take pleasure in the little boy's chatter and were in the habit of spoiling him a little, it seemed to Lee. Lee didn't care. He was just glad Danny's hearing finally seemed to be back to normal since the lightning strike. This morning, with Erica feeling a mite poorly, he'd made Danny ride with him for a while.

Even though James didn't need to speak the words, Lee knew he felt having Danny ride into Independence with them would seem "not right." Although Lee had ceased to notice the rich brown color of James and Erica's skin, he knew others might not treat them kindly. Like James had said the night before, "People still got the war on their minds and our kind are still thought of as slaves. Even though me and Erica have been free most of our lives. I sure hope we can join up on the same train as you. We'd miss the little feller if we had to say good-bye."

Lee knew, from talking to the couple, that they worried about having to travel on to California alone. There was still a lot of prejudice among southerners, and even many who had fought for the Union were leery around free blacks.

"The Richards are helpful, but we're gonna need a lot more help to get to California. A wagon train gives everyone a way to help each other in case we run into Indians or wagon trouble."

"Real Indians? Like Cherokee and Apache?"

"More like Kiowa and Sioux, I think." Lee tried to recall what little he'd read while holding tight to the reins. Easing the ox and wagon through the teeming streets made his head ache. Tied to the back of the wagon, Cletus tossed his head and snorted disapproval. Behind them, the Richards' two-mule team kept pace.

***

"Whoa!" For every inch he moved forward, he had to jerk on the reins to halt the ox as someone ran in front of them or another obstacle blocked his way.

"Will they scalp us?" Danny's eyes were wide in his face. Probably remembering all the lurid stories he read in forbidden dime novels.

"I don't think so—from what I've read, most of the tribes are peaceable these days." He didn't share with Danny what he'd read in the newspapers or talked with James about after the little boy had bedded down for the night. How some tribes resented the settlers cutting through their hunting grounds, fouling their watering holes, or destroying their traditions. While Lee could sympathize with their plight, he couldn't figure out another way to travel to California.

"Whoa! Whoa! Durn fool!" Lee yanked back on the reins as another loaded wagon lumbered from in front of a store and cut toward him. He'd be glad when they reached the outskirts of the town past the stockyards. An older man had advised James earlier that there was a train forming outside town.

"I talked to a man I met in the livery," James had said when they first entered the city. "There's a wagon train forming for the California Trail led by a man named Smith. The man said he's open to letting such as us travel along." Without James spelling it out, Lee understood the man would not discount them because of the color of their skin. He'd heard of many wagon masters who refused to allow even free men of color to travel with them. *Pretty unkind,* Lee thought. *Mr. Montgomery taught us to judge a man by his actions, not his color.*

By the time Lee stopped the wagon in a clearing near ten other wagons, his shoulders ached from yanking on the reins and a fierce headache pounded in his temples. He'd never been so glad to shove on the brake and climb stiff-legged from the hard wagon seat. He asked an older woman with gray hair where he could find Mr. Smith. With a smile, she pointed out a wagon a few down the line. "Him there, with the tan shirt and black trousers."

A lean, tall man with a head of dark hair stood near a wagon, writing on a sheaf of papers in his hand. He balanced the papers against a water barrel, licked the tip of a pencil, and scribbled a little more.

"Mr. Smith?" Lee walked up, lifted his hat in greeting, and smoothed back his blond hair. "I'm Lee Connors. A man at the livery told me and my friends we might be able to join up with your wagon train. We're bound for California."

The man turned clear, steady blue eyes and gazed at him up and down. His eyes roved back to Lee's wagon as if taking stock. Without saying a word, he appeared to size him up. When he did speak, around a slow, easy grin, he nodded at Danny standing by Lee's leg. "The little feller with you?"

"Yes, sir, that's my brother." It had gotten easier to say it in the months since they'd left the orphanage. Lee had written and mailed a letter about a month ago to Mr. Montgomery. He didn't know if he'd ever hear anything more from the man— unless they settled in California, and he got word back somehow. Danny was his responsibility now.

"Sure, we can take you on. I'll want to check over your wagon and your supplies first. But, if you're determined to make it, you will."

Lee wanted to make sure before he committed to the journey. He pointed back to James' wagon where the Richards sat silent and proud on the wagon seat. "My friends too? We travel together."

"Where are you from, son?"

"Mississippi."

"You bring your friends along too?"

Lee wondered if he might be asking if the Richards had been his family's slaves. "No, sir, we met on the trail. The

Richards are free and come from Ohio. They have their papers if you need to check them over."

The man stared at James, looked at Erica with a flicker of concern, but in the end his steady gaze judged their character. To Lee's satisfaction, he did not ask to see any papers but took him at his word. "Sure, they're welcome to join us. I'm Trevor Smith, the wagon master. Other leader's a man named Tad Marshall, but he usually does the scouting ahead. You'll meet him later."

"Thank you, sir," Lee held out his hand to shake. Mr. Smith seemed surprised but returned the gesture with a firm, strong grip of his own.

"You can stop your wagon here for now. We're going to be pulling out in a day or so. I'm checking over folks' supplies to see what they have. We have a sutler going along, but it's best if people have their own stuff. You can restock in town if you like. I generally like to have folks camp out for a night or two, to see how we all get along before we pull out. Like to get some hunting in too, make sure we have fresh game to start. You any good at hunting, Lee Connor?"

"Yes, sir, I'm a fair hand."

Thanks to Thomas.

It took a few hours to make camp. Danny was a big help getting Cletus and the ox out on picket ropes, while Lee built a campfire for Erica and settled their bed rolls under the wagon for the night. He and Danny had both grown used to sleeping under the stars or the wagon since they'd left the orphanage. With all their supplies there was no room in the wagon anyway.

James and Erica's wagon was pulled by two massive gray mules. James did not allow the little boy to help with them because of their mean-tempered dispositions and sharp teeth. James had shown Lee a healing wound on his leg where a mule had bitten almost to the bone. After he'd led them away from the camp to graze in a somewhat downtrodden patch of grass, he spoke in his quiet, cultured voice, "Kind of takes a bit of getting used to, don't it? All these people?"

Lee nodded. Even in the clearing, with the city a mile or so behind them but looming like a blot on the horizon, they could hear noise and sense a mass of people. "Maybe it will be better once we get back on the road."

Suddenly, the thought of adventure left a sour taste in his mouth. Even though he knew it wasn't possible, Lee wished himself and Danny back at the Mississippi Orphanage.

We were safe there. I wish... But there was no sense in wishing.

In a couple of days, they'd be headed to California. Thousands of miles away from the only home Lee had ever known.

Thomas, I'm scared.

Chapter Six

A little later, on his way to fill a bucket of water from an enormous well, Lee was startled when a pretty girl with butter-yellow hair and a shimmery dress gave him a bold wink as she strutted by. And was her face—painted? Shocked at the sight, he could only stop and stare.

A group of young men, standing nearby, laughed at his blushing face. Although Lee figured he was by no means totally innocent about soiled doves—at least, he had heard whispers in Natchez—he couldn't recall ever seeing such a bold woman.

One of the men chuckled and called in a teasing voice, "Hey, farm boy! How come mama let you loose in the big city?" The other young men joined in the laughter. One of the men grabbed the woman and pulled her into a tent. More raucous laughter. The woman squealed and Lee hurried away.

Red-faced with shame, although he didn't know why, Lee ignored them and carried the bucket of water to Erica. With Danny busy helping James and Erica starting supper, Lee felt at loose ends. The men's taunting riled him although he couldn't tell why. In the orphanage, he had never felt he needed acceptance.

Out here, he suddenly wanted to belong, to fit in with these men and be one of them. Although maybe not the man who'd pulled the painted lady into the tent. What would Mr. Montgomery or the ladies of the Sunday School say to that?

Lee watched the others from a distance, the easy, sure way they stood, cigarettes loose in the corner of their lips. Smoke curled up from their lips. One short, stocky man in an overlarge black hat took the cigarette between two fingers and used it to punctuate a story he was telling the others. They all laughed, and one slapped the stocky man on the back.

In a town before he'd met the Richards, Lee had bought the makings of a smoke. He had never smoked before. In fact, Mr. Montgomery switched any boy who tried to smoke corn shucks behind the barn. Even though he smoked a pipe, the director didn't want the boys to begin a habit the orphanage's providers would see as "abhorrent." Anything that slowed the funds they needed was considered sinful. Lee didn't even know why he'd taken some of his and Danny's fast-disappearing cash to purchase tobacco and a booklet of rolling paper.

Thomas always said when he got to be a man, he'd smoke.

Lee pulled the makings from the wagon. As if he'd practiced it every day, Lee walked close enough so the men could notice him. He pulled a cigarette paper from the small booklet of papers, shook out some Bull Durham loose-leafed tobacco, and turned it into a tidy roll. Pleased with the neat package, he pulled a match from the box in his pocket, scratched it across the sole of his boot, and lit the end of the cigarette. It burnt with a steady flame.

Not quite sure what to do, Lee glanced sideways and imitated one man. He put the cigarette between his lips and drew in a deep breath. To his complete disgust, the smoke went down his throat in a choking agony of coughing. His eyes filled with tears at the unexpected burning, his mouth flew open, and the cigarette dropped to the ground.

The young men watching him burst into loud, hateful laughter.

Shamed again, Lee turned away. He picked up the cigarette just as Trevor Smith walked from around the wagon. As if the wagon master could figure out the whole situation, he glared hard at the men and then turned to Lee. In a quiet tone, so the others couldn't overhear, his soothing voice said, "Don't try so hard, son. You don't need to show off for the likes of them."

"I-I'm n-not," Lee managed to choke out around his seared, raspy throat. As if he didn't care, he dropped the cigarette and ground his boot tip into it.

"Tell you what," Trevor continued, "I'm taking a few men out into the hills to do some hunting tomorrow. Maybe you'd like to come along. We'll get some game to begin the trip."

"Yes, I would." If there was one thing Lee knew how to do, it was to hunt. Thomas and Mr. Montgomery had taught him to use a gun well. Being able to find game to help feed the orphans was a skill worth practicing. Thomas made certain of Lee's skill all those years ago. They often went hunting and brought back rabbits, squirrels, even wild boar.

Maybe I can't smoke like a man, Lee thought, *but I sure enough can shoot like one.*

***

The bugle blared well before sunrise to wake them. Lee was up, ready for morning chores, while Danny yawned and dragged himself off his pallet under the wagon. Back on the trail, they had never started so early, but Lee knew from a speech Trevor gave the night before that this would be their standard rising hour—except on Sundays. Trevor had gathered all the people in the wagon train to explain his rules and what would be expected of each person—even the children. "We face months on a long, difficult trail," Trevor had cautioned. "If anyone wants to turn back, now's the time. It's going to take all of us working together to make it through some mighty rough, inhospitable land. You're going to be hungry and thirsty. Some days you'll feel like if you take another step, you'll just give in." He looked at each face, then said in a steady, determined voice, "We'll bury some of you along the trail. Not all of you will make it. If that seems harsh, I just want to be truthful. You'll follow my lead and Mr. Marshall's, or you'll be left to go it alone. Make your decision tonight."

Like we can make a different choice now.

"I'm still tired," Danny grumbled as he tugged on overalls and reached for his boots. "It ain't even light yet."

"You know what Mr. Smith told us last night. He's in charge and we follow the rules of the wagon train or go off on our own. It's not much different than listening to Mr. Montgomery back at the orphanage."

Danny grumbled but set about leading Cletus and their ox to the watering hole. Erica was already building a breakfast fire. She looked a touch pale and clammy, but she still gave them both her gentle smile. "Soon as you've done chores," she promised Danny, "I might have eggs for breakfast. James traded some work with a man in town last night."

After Erica's good breakfast, with a rare treat of eggs, Lee saddled Cletus and joined Trevor—along with a couple of the younger men who had laughed at his smoking mishap the day before. They would hunt for a few hours and come back to break camp for the first day on the road. Others left behind would yoke up the oxen or mules and prepare to head out. Lee looked forward to the day with both anticipation and apprehension.

It helped to focus on hunting, a chore he did well. Trevor, as he asked to be called, rode out with Lee into a stand of small hills along the banks of the Missouri River. They parted company and each went deeper into the wooded area. Lee didn't mind. Left alone, he and "Henry", as he called his rifle, soon had a brace of pheasants and a couple of big jackrabbits. The Henry repeating rifle had been a gift from Mr. Ewell at the Natchez Mercantile. While they were mostly used by the North during the war between the states, Mr. Ewell had purchased one from a trader, with a good cache of ammunition to boot. Lee considered it one of his prized possessions.

While waiting to meet up with Trevor again, Lee dismounted, tied Cletus to a tree with a bit of browse in reach, and pulled out his handy knife. Thomas had taught him to skin an animal, so he got right to work and soon had the task done.

"Well, now, look at you." Trevor sounded surprised as he rode up, three rabbit carcasses tied to his saddle. "You've already got yours skinned."

"I guess I'm used to doing everything for myself," Lee answered, tying his game to hang from the saddle horn and mounting Cletus for the ride back to camp. "When you're an orphan, you learn to make do and get the job done."

If he thought Trevor would comment about him being an orphan, Lee was surprised to find out it didn't seem to matter. Instead, he chuckled as they rode along. "The women in the train will sure be glad to have you along. You're faster and probably more efficient than some of those young blades we got signed on. You'll be a good man to have along on the trail."

Remembering his humiliation of the day before, Lee felt his face flame. *Skinning an animal don't make a man like smoking does.*

"So, Lee Connor," Trevor asked, "you got a gal left behind, waiting for you to make a fortune in California and send for her?"

"A gal?"

Trevor grinned and Lee realized the man was teasing, almost like Thomas might have done. "No, I—I never had much time for girls or courting. At the orphanage, we weren't allowed to keep company with anyone... I mean... I never..." Too flustered to explain, Lee stumbled over the words. "No, I don't have a gal."

"Well, there's time yet, you're young. You'll find a girl someday. Maybe even on the trail."

Again, Lee's face warmed and he bit a corner of his lip. *Has Trevor ever kissed a girl? Would it be impolite to ask him? Thomas would have answered my questions about women if he hadn't gone off to war.*

Back at the train, an older woman praised Lee as he handed her the freshly skinned and skillet-ready meat. "Ain't you the one! Look at those plump birds! Maybe you'll even get us a buffalo along the way."

Lee tried to think of that exciting possibility as he hurried to take his place on the wagon. James had hitched the ox up and had Cletus tied to the back. It was 7:00 in the morning. Time for the journey to begin for the day. Trevor blew the bugle, and the wagon wheels took their first cumbersome jolts toward the promised land.

Chapter Seven

"I'm sorry, Lee," Danny sobbed, standing before Lee, a contrite bundle of misery. "I didn't mean to do it! I didn't!"

Lee stared down at the sodden mess of matches—*all* their matches for the trip—on the muddy ground at his feet. A sigh came up from his chest as he tried to control his temper. He couldn't really be angry at the young boy, not when he'd told Danny to carry a bucket of water to help James. Still, they were three days out from Independence and he had no matches.

Danny could have been more careful in not trying to carry the matches *and* the bucket of water at the same time, but Lee knew accidents happened. Danny hadn't planned to trip and spill the water over the scattered tin of matches. "It's okay, Danny. We'll figure out something. Sooner or later, we'll come to a fort. Maybe we can buy more there."

"I can ask James," Danny sniffed, wiping tears and snot from his dust-smudged face with the sleeve of a worn cotton shirt.

"No!"

Lee didn't mean to sound so sharp, but he'd seen the contents of James and Erica's wagon many times. Their small hoard of supplies was in danger of running out long before they made it to California. It worried him, but James was too proud to accept charity.

"No, Danny," he kept his voice quiet and put an arm around the boy's shoulder. Gave him a steady hug. "They have even less than we do. We can't impose. But maybe there's someone else who could make a trade with us. I'll ask around. Don't you worry, now."

At noon that day, when they pulled the wagons to a stop to make camp for nooning, Lee had a chance to ask Trevor.

"You can buy from Freddy Scott; he's got a supply," Trevor said as he helped a widow woman named Mrs. Evans unyoke her oxen. "He's the sutler I told you about. He often sells to people on the road. Although I must warn you, he charges twice what you'd pay in a town."

Twice! Although Lee had been careful with the twenty-dollar gold piece and the collection his neighbors had taken up for him, money sure didn't seem to last long.

"I'd hoped to make a trade," Lee said, "It seems kind of selfish to me, charging folks more."

"Haw!" Trevor shouted to the oxen as he pulled them left and led them a short distance from the wagon to graze. "Maybe so," he agreed as he pounded the picket post into the ground with a wooden mallet. Wiped sweat from his forehead with a dull red kerchief. "But Scott's traveled this trail many times—not with me—I've not dealt with the man before. Didn't really want to deal with him this time but didn't have any choice. He can be handy, others tell me. He loads a wagon with supplies and sells them on the trail. Digs for gold awhile in California and then goes back east to restock. It can be helpful. Someone told me he has a family back in Arkansas, but they've never traveled with him far as I know."

"Where will I find him?"

Trevor pointed out Freddy Scott, a stout, balding man with a large Conestoga wagon behind a yoke of six oxen. To Lee's disgust, he watched Freddy joking with the girl he'd seen taken into the man's tent before leaving Independence. Hanna, her name was. Erica had told him in whispers what the other women on the train said about the girl.

"Mrs. Evans told me about her," Erica explained one evening after Danny had been bedded down. "Her name's Hanna Miller. She's a German bound for California to strike it rich in the gold fields. A woman! If you can call her that— no decent lady would."

"Now, Erica," James admonished, sitting down to pull a tin coffee pot off the fire with a cross-stitched dish towel. He poured coffee into a mug and handed it to Lee. Filled his own mug before he admonished, "Gossip's a sin."

Erica stiffened up and glared across the campfire at her husband. "It's not gossip! Mrs. Evans is a respectable woman, traveling alone with a young son, so she's got to be careful. That Miller woman's not polite for decent company. Why she doesn't even have a wagon!"

Lee had noticed this early on the trail. How Hanna, all her worldly goods packed on a horse and mule, pitched a tent each night. Although gossip on the train was that she rarely slept there. Holding his mug of coffee, his face flushed when he thought of what she might be doing instead. *The world sure was a different place than the orphanage.*

"I just want you to know, Lee. Best keep little Danny away from her. Even though the rest of us try to wash up—hard enough with all this dust blowing at us night and day—I've never seen the woman take so much as a soapy cloth to her face. When she came up to ask me if I had any saleratus she could borrow—there was..." As if the word were too awful to speak, she lowered her voice to just a bare whisper. "There was vermin in her hair! Lice!"

With that distressing thought in mind, Lee walked toward Freddy Scott's wagon. Before he got there, Hanna sauntered off, swishing the skirt of a green silk dress as if asking for attention. Lee breathed a sigh of relief. It didn't look right that Mr. Scott was talking to a woman like that. Hadn't Trevor said Mr. Scott had a family in Arkansas? Well, Lee decided, ashamed of jumping to conclusions, maybe Hanna had to buy something, just like him.

"Mr. Scott?"

"Freddy, call me Freddy." The man seemed jovial enough as he held out a limp hand to grab Lee's. "We're all in the same wagon train, no strangers here. You're Lee Connor, traveling with the j–"

Before he could say anything bad about Erica and James, Lee cut him off. "Yes, sir," Calling the man "sir" grated on his mind, though.. He didn't think much of Freddy Scott so far. Maybe it was his too-cheerful face, the way his lips twisted in his flabby cheeks and came out with the worst-sounding insults. Words Lee had certainly never heard in polite company. Every evening around the campfire, Freddy had one tale after another that insulted someone. "I'd like to buy a tin of matches. Unless you'd consider a trade."

"Trade?" Freddy threw back his head with a loud guffaw. "What use would a trade do me, young fella? I've got a wagon load of goods and need cash to buy more. Be glad to sell you a tin of matches, though." He quoted a price that caused Lee's face to blanch. *Robbery!* But Lee had to have matches, or else wait until others built a fire for each meal and carry a torch to light his own. That would get tedious fast. He didn't like to be beholden to anyone.

A few minutes later, Lee, his coin pouch noticeably emptier, carried the matches back to his wagon. This time, he carefully put them into a tin box. On the way back to his wagon, he couldn't help glance back at Mr. Scott. A couple of the men Erica called "trouble," were standing nearby, talking in low voices. Lee didn't know why he felt uneasy, but he did.

***

"Hey, Lee," Danny called out about a week later. The boy had been walking alongside the wagon as he did most days. Surprisingly, Danny's crooked leg worked to his advantage over the hard, uneven ground. Women and children walked to give the animals less of a load to pull. Lee often wished Danny were big enough to drive, so he could walk too. "Look up ahead. Don't that look like a wagon on the trail?"

From his bumpy, jolting seat on the wagon, Lee pushed his wide brimmed hat back and shaded his eyes. Sure enough, it looked like a wagon camped by the side of the trail.

Since leaving Kansas behind, they'd gone into Wyoming Territory. Lee tried not to think of all the miles that lay ahead. *Why would someone be sitting on the side of the trail all alone? Sure is a mighty lonely place to sit.*

Today, Lee had gotten the lead wagon position. With all the dust churned up by the wagons, everyone took turns being in front. Yesterday, Lee and Danny had been the last wagon in line—a miserable, hot, dust-choking journey. Lee was glad when Trevor blew the bugle to set up camp last night. It had been the longest eleven hours he'd ever traveled.

He and Danny were in a perfect spot to spy the wagon up ahead. As the wagon jolted closer over the rutted road, Trevor rode past on his jet-black stallion to scout ahead.

"I'm going to see what's going on," Trevor said as he rode by. "Wait until I signal you to come or stay. It's likely all right, or Tad would have ridden back to let us know earlier. But, just in case, wait here."

They watched as he stopped near the wagon, dismounted, and walked over to talk to someone sitting beside a campfire. A motion from his hand showed Lee it was all right to keep moving forward.

Trevor came riding back. "It's a young woman. She's all alone. A spoke in her wagon wheel cracked, so Tad told her we'd camp here for the night and help. Go ahead and circle your wagon up past hers. I'll let the others know." After Lee's nod, Trevor rode back to pass the word along to the rest of the wagons.

"Early camp tonight!" Danny hollered. He skipped along ahead with several of the other children from the wagon train. Anything new or different was exciting to them after so many humdrum days on the road. They turned around and went on down the line of wagons, passing along the news to the other twenty-five wagons in the train. To Lee's delight, but probably not to many of the others', Danny's hearing had come all the way back to normal. It meant his little-boy voice could shout or holler or tease like any of the other chattering children in the train.

Lee glanced at the woman's camp as he drove the ox on past, circling his wagon so the others could settle in behind him. He caught only a glimpse of her as he drove past—long dark hair held back with a limp blue ribbon, curvy and tall, wearing a pale blue dress. Looked awful young to be out here all alone.

Lee wondered, briefly, what her story might be, but he had to tend to the business of unhitching the ox, seeing the animals were staked out with food and grain. Making camp took work before he could sit down for the evening meal and rest for a spell. In the past few weeks, he'd practiced rolling himself a cigarette and smoking while he did evening chores.

It helped calm him, and the scent of tobacco could be pleasant. More pleasant than the buffalo chips the women and children picked up as they walked to light the evening fires. He didn't give much thought to the woman until a few minutes later when he heard a commotion near her wagon.

"Stop! Let me alone!"

Chapter Eight

"Leave me alone!"

Startled, Lee sat down the bucket of water he'd been carrying to start a pot of coffee. *Where's Trevor?* As the wagon master, he should be the one dealing with any trouble on the train. Lee sighed. From where he stood, he could see "the outlaws", as he called the younger men who made fun of his smoking and caused general devilment at times, trying to grab at the girl. They were shoving her from man to man like a plaything, and Freddy Scott had left his wagon behind to laugh with the rest of them.

The man who'd taken Hanna into a tent in Independence reached out an impertinent hand to brush a brown curl from the girl's face. She turned beseeching blue eyes in Lee's direction. Fearful and uncertain. In that moment, he saw only a young girl—like his sisters at the orphanage—being mistreated.

Freddy stepped forward and shoved the man away from the girl. "Move aside, you tadpole," he chuckled in his deep, belly laugh, his fat hands ready to paw her. "The lady needs a man, not a boy. Isn't that right, little lady? How'd you like to come visiting in my wagon for a little while?"

How dare he?

Lee was good with his hands, not with his fists. There were more of the "outlaws" than of him, and some of them were larger to boot. It sure was easier when the bullies in life were the younger boys at the orphanage. How could he help this girl out of her predicament?

Guess it's time to find out.

Lee clenched his lips over the smoldering cigarette and tromped over to the woman. With more bravery than he felt—his legs couldn't stop trembling—he shoved Freddy Scott away from the girl. He stumbled back and almost lost his balance.

"Hey, you!" The man's face went livid with an angry flush.

"Stay away from her!" Lee shouted as he pulled out the cigarette and tossed it to the ground. He reached out, grabbed the girl around the waist and pulled her close to his side. Until he spoke, Lee had no idea what he'd say. "This is my... my betrothed! She's been waiting here for me. You leave her alone!"

Freddy's dark eyes squinted like an angry boar's. "Liar! You don't know this girl."

The girl struggled a little in Lee's arms, trying to pull away, but he held her still. He had some idea what had happened to Hanna in the one man's tent, and he didn't want this girl to be used the same way. Looking into her cornflower, blue eyes, he gave her a stern, warning look. A you-better-behave glance he'd used on the little girls at the orphanage. Although she trembled in his arms, she kept her lips stitched tight. Those eyes, though, spit fire.

"Yes, I do. We've been writing to one another, and she was supposed to wait along the trail for me." *Only don't ask me her name because I don't know it! What might a man call his sweetheart?*

"What's the trouble here?" Too late, Trevor showed up.

Trembling, Lee held the girl tighter against his side, felt her labored breathing and the way she quivered like a small animal in a trap.

"Lee here says this is his betrothed—waiting on the trail for him," Freddy sputtered. "I don't believe him."

Trevor looked at them both, studying Lee's face and the girl's. "This true, Lee? Nancy?"

So that was her name!

"Yes, Nancy and I have been writing to one another. We planned to meet up on the trail." Lee stated, remembering his conversation with Trevor the day they'd gone hunting. Trevor knew he didn't have a girl waiting for him. What would he do? Would he laugh and force Lee to tell the truth?

The "outlaws" made rude comments but seemed to be losing interest. When Trevor told them to get back to their own wagons, most of them turned and swaggered off, grumbling among themselves. Freddy remained, squinty eyes glaring, his lips pressed tight.

"I don't believe it," Freddy said in a disagreeable tone. "I say if you're betrothed, then kiss the girl."

Kiss the girl? Here? Now?

Lee stood frozen in place, aware that some of the other men had turned around at Freddy's suggestion and were snickering at his obvious discomfort. *Kiss?* He knew that when people kissed their lips pressed. He'd seen James and Erica kiss a few times on the trail. It looked so natural—but then, they'd been married for seven years.

"Seems like a reasonable request," Trevor winked, probably knowing Lee had made the whole thing up to protect the girl. Just like Thomas' would have, his words goaded Lee to action. *He knows I'm lying.*

Kiss, in front of... in front of everyone? He'd never expected his first kiss would happen with an audience of people. To a girl he didn't even know!

Kiss? His stomach churned and his heartbeat like a drummer in his chest. Before he lost his nerve, Lee bent his head down as he gazed into those blue, blue eyes and he pressed his lips to Nancy's in a chaste kiss. To his surprise, she tasted sweet, lips soft and moist under his. Beneath his hands, Nancy stood as stiff as stone. Astonished, Lee didn't want to pull away. When Trevor spoke, Lee jerked away, startled. *So that's a kiss.*

"Welcome to our wagon train, Nancy," Trevor said. "Any friend of Lee's is a friend of mine. Come on, Freddy, let's leave those two alone. I imagine they're got a lot of catching up to do."

Although Freddy mumbled and gave them both a suspicious glance, he turned and walked back to his wagon. The rest of the crowd followed too. Lee could only be glad Danny hadn't been around to witness his lying and the kiss— *that kiss!* Trevor gave him a knowing wink. In minutes, he and Nancy stood alone beside her wagon.

A brief smile crossed his face as he remembered those soft lips beneath his–

Slap!

Nancy's hand came up to smack him hard on the face.

"Hey, what's that for?" Lee asked, holding a hand to his stinging cheek. "I just protected your honor. Is that any way for a future wife to act?" He tried to make a joke about it but the anger in Nancy's eyes stopped him. Lee gulped, suddenly seeing the whole thing from Nancy's side. Even though the "outlaws" and Freddy had tried to assault her, he'd been just as bad—kissing her without her permission. As if she were no better than a woman like Hanna.

"I'm ..." he started to apologize when an elderly lady in a gray dress and a tattered white shawl hurried up to him. He'd met the McGregors on the first day on the trail and liked the older couple, even if they did often need help in the simplest things.

"Lee," Greta McGregor spoke in her usual flustered fidget, a mirthful smile curving her pink cheeks and twinkling in her blue eyes. "I don't mean to bother you, but could you help Mr. McGregor water our animals tonight? His shoulder is bothering him too badly to lift the buckets. If you could?"

"Sure, Mrs. McGregor." Then realizing his manners, he introduced the two women. "Mrs. McGregor, this is Nancy..."

For the first time she spoke in a normal voice, lovely and sweet. "Fitzgerald. Nancy Fitzgerald."

The older woman reached out for one of Nancy's long, pale hands. "So pleased to meet you, deary. Aren't you just the prettiest thing? Look, Lee, at those dark eyebrows and those blue eyes!" The woman ran her gnarled fingers through Nancy's dark curls. "And that pretty hair! How do you keep your skin so nice and white out here? You must wear a sunbonnet and veil every hour of the day!"

Lee couldn't stop looking at the girl's pale face.

"Well, now, you come with Lee and we'll talk while he waters the animals. I've got a pot of beans near about ready for supper and we'll tell our stories. I'd sure like to know how a young woman such as yourself got out here. Word's out you're Lee's betrothed. So glad to meet you."

Greta led Nancy back to her campfire and introduced her to Mr. McGregor. "This is Eugene. We've been married nigh on thirty-five years, isn't that right, husband?"

"Aye," Eugene agreed, pulling a well-worn corncob pipe from between his pursed lips. "Come a'courting when I was just a lad. Got married when I were twenty-two. Greta there was just a babe. Seventeen, she was. How old might you be, Miss Fitzgerald?"

"Eighteen."

"Ah, a good age," he winked. "Sit down, sit down."

Lee went to water the McGregor's' animals and came back to find Nancy, a plate of food in her lap and Greta fussing over her like a child. "Now, you eat that all down. Lee, you sit and eat too. I saw Danny's gone to eat with the Richards, so you don't have to worry about him. Danny is Lee's brother," Greta informed Nancy as she motioned him to sit on a log beside her. "But I expect you know that already."

A little uncomfortable on the log—sitting shoulder-to-shoulder with a girl was a new experience—Lee sat and held out his hand for the tin plate of beans and hoe cake Greta handed him.

The spry little woman sat in a rocking chair she'd brought from home, folded her hands across the lap of her gray dress, and gave them both a knowing look. "Puts you in mind of us, don't it now," she chuckled to her husband, "young and just starting out."

Lee flushed and spooned up beans, in a hurry to have this awkward meal over. Beside him, Nancy shifted on the log and seemed to have the same trouble eating.

"Now, wife," Eugene cautioned as he held out a mug for a refill of coffee, "you leave them be." He addressed the next words to Lee and Nancy. "Greta likes to play matchmaker with any young folks she sees. Wants them to be as happy as we've been."

Unexpectedly, Nancy spoke up, "And you have been—happy?" There was a quiver in her voice Lee couldn't understand, almost a yearning. *Did she have a fellow somewhere waiting? Or did she have a husband who had abandoned her on the trail?* Suddenly, he lost his appetite. Greta's beans tasted bland and mushy in his mouth. When he swallowed, it was over a lump in his throat.

Greta's green eyes shone as she looked at Eugene over the sparks shooting up from the campfire. "Oh, my, yes! Never a quarrel or disagreement."

In a quiet voice, almost a whisper, Lee heard Nancy say, "I always kind of hoped..."

Later, he could never say why, but Lee reached out his hand, took the hand she laid loosely on the skirt of her blue dress, and squeezed gently. *What have you done?* He expected another slap. Instead, Nancy turned to him in the dusk, those cornflower blue eyes moist with unshed tears and a timid smile quivering on her lips. To his complete surprise, she gave him a gentle squeeze back.

It was too early to ask Nancy her secrets, but Lee found himself eager to know her story.

Chapter Nine

"How about a shooting contest?"

Having an early camp was almost like a holiday, or a Sunday. With Nancy's wagon wheel needing a day to repair, Trevor decided they'd all stop an extra day to do any necessary repairs. They'd soon be facing harsher conditions. Now was the time to reorganize their supplies, lighten the loads if needed, and prepare for the trail ahead.

"It's important to keep up spirits on any train," Trevor explained to Lee as they rested over a meal of Erica's hoe cakes and beans the next morning. "It takes so long to travel to California, it's good to take a rest now and then so folks don't get too weary along the way. Most of the wagon wheels need to be greased. Animals need to rest and we're in a good place to camp."

"You won't get an argument from me," Lee agreed after he swallowed Erica's warm hoecakes, covered in butter from the McGregor's cows. Eugene milked their two cows every morning and shared the milk with others on the train. Any extra, he put in a bucket that hung beneath the wagon as they rode over the trail. By the end of the day, the jolting of the wagon had "churned" the butter. Lee had never expected to have such a luxury on the trail.

"A day spent wisely now," Trevor said, "might mean less trouble in the rugged wilderness ahead. Like what happened to your intended." He winked from behind a mug of coffee as if he'd known all along Lee had never met her before.

They spent the morning working on repairs and chores and while everyone was sitting around resting at nooning, someone called out, "How about a shooting contest?"

Lee didn't know who first proposed the idea, but several of the men hollered their enthusiasm.

"Sounds fine!"

"Sure, enough! You in, Lee?"

"Sure, count me in," Lee answered, eager to stop all the questions he'd fended from others on the trains since the night before. They all wanted to know about one thing— Nancy. *Like I know more than they do.*

Danny, eager to show off Lee's skills, went around and collected empty tin cans to use as targets.

"I bet Lee wins," Danny bragged to his new friend, Mark Evans, another young boy traveling with his widowed mother. "He's a right good shot an' he's got a new rifle too."

"Betcha he don't," Mark argued just because. The boys had become fast friends and walked alongside Lee's wagon most days. "Betcha Freddy Scott wins. I heard someone say he's come along on five or six wagon journeys, and he wins near about every time."

"Who told you that?"

Mark shrugged. "Somebody, don't rightly know."

Danny was so worried about the outcome that he followed Lee to the edge of the camp where the men had decided to set up a shooting gallery – an old log with a line of tin cans. "Lee, you're a right good shot, aren't you?"

"Good enough." He pulled the Henry rifle from the scabbard and made sure it was loaded. Although he didn't like wasting ammunition, he figured, like Trevor, that a contest was good for the train's spirits. And maybe... just maybe Nancy would notice what a good shot he was. Lee blushed.

I sure would like to know how she got left on the trail.

No one seemed to know Nancy's story. Even Mrs. McGregor admitted to being unable to learn more about the strange girl. Nancy kept to herself and didn't talk much. When the older woman prodded Lee for more information about his betrothed, he mumbled how it was up to Nancy to tell what she wanted known. *And maybe one day she'll tell me too.* Trying not to blurt out the truth got harder by the second. *I never saw Nancy before in my life!*

"Okay, everyone," Trevor hollered out the rules. "Each man gets six shots. Shoot all the cans down and you move to the next round. Shoot another six cans, we'll move back another five paces. We shoot until only one man is left. Let's draw straws to see who goes first."

"I sure hope you win," Danny worried as Lee got in line behind one of the "outlaws" who had drawn a broom straw for first shot. "I bet Mark you would. If you win, he has to do my chores for two nights. If that old Freddy Scott wins, I got to do his chores."

"Danny!" Lee hadn't found many times he had to be firm with his brother on the trip, but now seemed like a good time. "Betting is wrong. This is all fun, there's no betting going on. If I win, you'll do your own chores."

"But, Lee... " the boy protested. "What about Mark?"

Pop! Pop! Pop! Pop!

"Aw, too bad!" The shouts rang out. The "outlaw"—Lee had learned this one's name was Spence—had left two cans standing. "Better luck next time! Who's up next?"

"Lee! Lee Connor!"

There was no time to tell Danny he meant what he said. Taking a deep breath, Lee stepped up to the line someone had drawn in the dirt.

"Okay, Lee," Trevor explained the rules. "You'll shoot six cans from this distance. If you get them all, you'll move back five feet more and shoot again. If you miss any the first round, you're out."

"Like Spence!" someone joked. The crowd mumbled, laughed, and then quieted as Lee stepped up to the mark. He'd already loaded the Henry. Lifting it up to eye level, he sighted on the target, took a deep breath, and shot.

Pop! Pop! Pop! Pop! Pop! Pop!

All six cans toppled and sailed off the log in a neat row. The crowd cheered. All except Freddy Scott. He stepped up for his turn at the first distance. "Just beginner's luck," he grumbled. "You won't make it in the next round. Now watch some fine shooting."

Although Freddy's choice of weapons was a Colt six-shooter, he managed to down all six cans too.

The crowd cheered for him. Trevor's cowboy boots marked off five paces back. "Now, we'll shoot from this distance. Same rules. Whoever gets the most cans down, wins. If you both get all the cans down, we'll move back five more paces. Lee, you're first."

Again, Lee stepped up to the line in the dirt. At the far edge of the crowd, he noticed Nancy's long brown curls blowing in a slight breeze. Today she wore a brown dress sprigged with yellow flowers. In her hand she held a wildflower she'd picked from the trail. Although he couldn't be certain, not with the sun glaring down, he thought she gave him a timid smile from beneath a brown sunbonnet.

ZACHARY MCCRAE

Taking a deep breath, he once again shot at the tin cans. Again, all six went sailing off the log. Danny's loud whoops of delight shattered the air.

"Beginner's luck," Freddy grumbled as he passed Lee to take his own turn. Cocky, too sure of himself, Freddy raised the Colt, aimed, and shot. Five of the cans fell from the log. The sixth shot went wild and pierced into the wood below the can. For just a moment, everyone stood so still they could hear the oxen lowing near the creek and a bird call in the cloudless blue sky overhead.

"Lee Connor wins!" Trevor shouted.

Some of the group rushed up to congratulate Lee. "Nice shooting, Lee!" "Right smart eye there, young fella!"

Danny whooped and hollered, dancing around in a jig until he was in danger of losing his overalls when a strap broke. Mark, lower lip out in a pout, glared and stomped off. Lee figured he'd have to have a talk with both boys about betting. When he glanced toward where he'd seen Nancy, he saw to his disappointment that she'd walked away.

"Congratulations, Lee," James Richards said as he walked up to shake Lee's hand. "You're a fine shot."

As James stood beside him, Freddy rudely pushed the dark-skinned man out of his way. Freddy had been clear from the start about what he thought of having "slaves" along on the trip. "Beginner's luck," he said again in a sour voice. "No kid can shoot better than a man. We'll try this again another day, boy." The *boy* was almost a sneer.

Lee chose to ignore it and started to walk away with James, face taut, lips pressed tight against what he'd like to say to Freddy.

"Another thing," Freddy spoke low enough only Lee could hear him. In a nasty voice, seething with insinuation, he said, "You might fool some, but you aren't fooling me. I know you and that girl aren't betrothed. You never saw her before in your life. You better watch your step, boy."

Lee knew it was a warning. Of what, he couldn't be certain.

***

Nancy strolled along the grassy clearing, coming across rocky ruts where wagon trails had gone before. Although she'd stopped to watch the shooting contest earlier, she just wanted to be alone for a while to get her thoughts in order.

I'm not alone anymore.

Nancy wasn't quite sure how many days it had been since Uncle abandoned her along the trail. She wasn't entirely sure where she even was. She knew they'd been in Kansas at one point because he told her so. Where he'd left her, she didn't know. She only knew she sat for three long, quiet, soul-searing days while the sun beat down and rolled across the sky to nightfall. On the morning of the fourth day, she'd gotten up, broken camp, hitched Beauty to the wagon and plodded onward. West. Hoping eventually, she'd come to a town. A town with a telegraph office where she could contact Mr. Morgan to come get her. If he would.

Would he?

Mr. Smith and Mr. Maxwell seem kind. Allowing me to join their wagon train.

Nancy told him Uncle had ridden off to scout ahead. He had not come back even though she waited. When she traveled on, the wagon wheel cracked. Although Nancy did not often give in to despair, she'd felt then the world might as well end. She would sit there and die when her supplies ran out. The coyotes would feast on her bones.

Do they believe my story? Mr. Smith seemed to think something bad had happened to Uncle. He'd offered to let the men on his train fix her wheel, to allow her to travel with them. Nancy knew she should be grateful, but another part of her wished she could afford to turn his help down. If she'd been strong enough to put on a new wheel, she would never have stopped and prayed for help to come. It was annoying to feel so helpless. When Mama had died, Nancy had vowed she would never be as helpless as Mama—but look how far that got her.

"How do there." A tall, thin woman in a threadbare yellow poplin walked up to Nancy. Her hand held tight to a small, blond boy about seven. His face wore a pout and his dark blue eyes studied Nancy with mistrust. "You must be Nancy. Greta told me you'd joined our train. I'm Josephine Evans and this here is my son, Mark."

"I'm pleased to meet you, Mrs. Evans." *Or I reckon I am.* Nancy often found it hard to talk to other women in town. Living so isolated on Uncle's farm didn't give her much experience in talking like a regular person and Uncle didn't encourage friendships he didn't approve. Uncle rarely approved of anyone.

"Oh, call me Josie—everybody does."

"I don't," Mark grumbled around a mutinous pucker of his lips. "I ain't never called you Josie."

The woman gave him a stern shake. "Now, Mark, you stop that, you hear?" Turning to Nancy, she gave her a wink from sea-blue eyes. "He's angry because his friend's brother won the shooting contest. Lee Connor? He's just the nicest man we got along with us. But, I reckon you know that. Always helping. He comes from Mississippi and lived in an orphans' home his entire life. Although, I reckon you know that too. Greta says you're betrothed an' Mr. Smith says your uncle brought you out here and then something happened to him? My ain't you a brave one! Staying all alone to wait for Lee!"

Well, that was interesting. Nancy often felt like an orphan herself with Mama and Papa both gone. Lee Connor seemed like a nice enough man. Nicer than those terrible men who had pawed her and said wicked things. Again, Nancy's heart sank as she thought of the names Uncle had called her. *But what made them treat me like that? Maybe I really am that kind of woman? Maybe I'm not fit to speak to a decent woman like this Josie.*

"Will you excuse me," Nancy stopped Josie from prattling on more information about others in the wagon train. "This sun is quite hot. I feel a little... a little faint."

"Well, now, you best go see Greta McGregor," Josie said. "She knows every potion there is to help you out."

"Thank you, thank you." Nancy turned abruptly and hurried away from the woman's knowing eyes. *What would she say if she knew the kind of woman I am? Would she want me near her little boy?*

Before Nancy could stumble back to the protection of her wagon, although she couldn't go inside with the men still carving a new wagon spoke, Freddy Scott approached her. She knew him by name now. Greta McGregor had been sure to warn her the night before.

"He's a bad one, he is," Greta whispered, "you stay away from his kind. Hear tell he has a family back in Arkansas but he's never brung any of them along on his selling trips. Takes up with... wicked women..." Greta's round face flushed as if the words were too shameful to even think.

Nancy's heart quailed inside as Freddy stepped in front of her, blocking her path.

Chapter Ten

"Excuse me, please, I'm going to my wagon."

"Is that so?" He sneered at her in a way that made Nancy's skin crawl. "I know a secret. Would you like to hear it?"

"No. Let me pass!" Nancy stepped to the side of the trail in the hopes of getting away. Her high buttoned shoes twisted on a loose pile of stones, and she fought for balance. The man cornered her again and grabbed the sleeve of her brown poplin. Beneath his tight fingers, she felt the old familiar tension in her stomach, the same she'd felt before a beating from Uncle. "Let—me—go!"

"Ah, a little spitfire, are we?" he taunted as Nancy struggled to yank herself free.

"Well, I'm going to tell you my secret anyway." His leering face, smelling of cigar smoke and onions, pressed to her hot cheek. "I know you and Lee are not betrothed. You didn't even know one another until yesterday. And if you don't belong to him, I'd say you are free for the taking."

He thinks I'm one of those women! The ones people whisper about and call names like Uncle did. How does he know?

"What's going on here? Are you all right, Nancy?" Lee Connor stood off to the side, hand on a Henry repeating rifle.

Nancy had never been so relieved to see anyone in her life. Not even when she'd seen the dust from the wagon train the other day and knew rescue was at hand had she felt such a soaring of hope in her heart.

"Ah," Freddy sneered, but he dropped his tight grip on her arm. "It's the bridegroom to be, is it? Come to rescue his damsel in distress?"

"Leave her be, Freddy."

"Or what?"

"Leave her be," Lee repeated, boots planted firmly by Nancy's side. The dark blue of his pants pressed against the skirt of her brown poplin but Nancy did not step away. In her heart, she knew this man would not harm her or treat her like the others had so far.

Although Freddy grumbled and whispered a few choice words, he turned a cold eye on them and left them alone. Nancy realized her heart had been hammering inside the bodice of her brown dress like a pounding tinsmith. Her breath came in ragged spurts. The tight ball of her stomach began to ease back to normal.

"T-thank you for coming to my rescue."

Lee tipped a wide-brimmed hat of brown felt. "I don't like to see anyone mistreated. He had no right to treat a lady that way."

A lady? He thought she was a lady? *Could it be? He didn't see a...* The words were too shameful even to think.

Nancy thought about the kiss the night before. She had never been kissed before—not by a man. Although she'd been surprised, it hadn't been altogether unpleasant. Even this morning it troubled her that she could look at his firm, strong lips and wish he might kiss her again. *Does that make me a wayward woman? To think such things and desire them? If I want Lee to kiss me, what would Mr. Morgan think?*

It had lasted mere seconds, but Nancy couldn't forget how it had made her feel. Cherished and... loved? How did you know what love felt like? How did you know enough to be married as long as the McGregors? Could she have that when she got to California?

"I could walk you back to your wagon," he was saying, giving her a curious glance with those green eyes. Nancy thought they were the warmest green eyes she'd ever seen.

"Oh, yes, please!" If she sounded too eager, so be it!

He didn't take her arm but turned to walk beside her. Nancy knew they would have only minutes before they reached the edge of the wagons, circled for the night, and the curious eyes of the other people making supper or checking over supplies. It was time to express what she'd thought of last night. When he so sweetly squeezed her hand. *Had that been wrong too?*

"I wanted to thank you for yesterday too, for coming to my rescue. I don't know why those men..."

Nancy knew she couldn't tell him what she'd struggled over through a long, sleepless night. She knew why those men had taunted her, fondled her. It was because Uncle was right, and she was a wanton woman.

"You're welcome." He said the words in a gentle voice, a pleasant voice.

Nancy wasn't used to a man's voice being pleasant or even-tempered. Uncle's voice either barked, hollered, or swore. It grated on Nancy's nerves and made her clumsy-fingered and unsteady on her feet. Lee's voice was soothing, comforting, and gentle. She could see him as an orphan, talking to those children as an older brother. So sweetly.

She knew she had no right to ask him. He had no obligation to help her in the least. But after this fresh encounter with Freddy Scott, Nancy knew she would need protection to reach Mr. Morgan. It seemed wrong to use Lee Connor to reach her husband-to-be, but necessary. He seemed an honorable man.

"Mr. Connor?"

"Lee. Please, call me Lee."

"Lee." Now why did that name taste so pleasant on her tongue? "I know I have no right to ask such a thing. And you are to feel no obligation to help me. But I have a feeling I will need protection on this journey. If I'm to reach California unmolested, it might be better..." *How can you ask him this thing?* Fresh waves of guilt washed through her, and she almost couldn't form the words. Her throat tightened in agony.

Why must it be that women need men to protect them? Why can't I do everything myself? It grates to be so—so dependent upon a man. If Mama hadn't had to depend on Uncle, she would still be alive.

"Never mind, I have no right to ask you."

"If I could keep pretending to be your betrothed?" He helped her out in his quiet way.

Nancy's relief was so great she stopped in the path and reached a hesitant hand out to touch the sleeve of his dark blue linen shirt. His arm felt warm and muscled beneath her fingers. A blush warmed her cheeks. "Oh, yes, if you could! I would want you to feel no obligation once we reach California—but only . . ."

He studied her with those calm, thoughtful eyes and her heart sank. Of course, he would not want to be compelled to help a woman such as herself. He probably knew all about her. Maybe he felt she would allow him to take liberties if they were betrothed.

Then he smiled. It was a kind smile, showing a gap between his teeth that gave him a boyish look. Although he probably wouldn't like to hear it, those straight white teeth with the funny little gap made him look years younger. *Innocent. Yes, that was the right word to describe Lee Connor.*

Although that kiss hadn't been entirely innocent, not when it stirred her heart in such a funny way. He was a man, almost like all the others, but he would not treat her as the other men had. Nancy didn't understand how she knew, but her heart told her it was fine to trust him.

Oh, please!

Chapter Eleven

Nebraska

Near the Platte River

"How many miles to California?" Nancy mumbled to Lee's ox, as she snapped the harness and urged the lumbering animal along the rocky path. No one could hear her with all the other noises flowing around in the heat-laden afternoon, but she didn't really expect an answer anyway. "Guess talking to myself helps pass the time. Right, Charlie?"

Wagons creaked and groaned, the metal rims of the wheels hitting the rocks with a jarring noise that grated the ear. The oxen lowed and the horses with riders clopped along in easy rhythm. Children ran alongside the wagons, laughing, playing games to brighten their day. A small smile lifted Nancy's face as Lee's little brother, Danny, ran by waving a big stalk of some weed like a flag.

"Can't catch me," he taunted to little Mark Evans running to catch up. "I'm faster than you!"

Sure wish I could be out walking.

Driving fifth wagon in line, Nancy sighed as she bumped on the hard, wooden wagon seat, feeling every jolt and jar of the road. If there'd been anyone else to drive her wagon, she'd have been glad to walk along as some of the women and children did. They made it almost a picnic, laughing, talking, picking wildflowers, or gathering herbs. "A 'course," Nancy said to herself and Charlie, "I've never had many friends. Not with Uncle around."

In the week since she'd joined the train, Nancy had spoken to some of the other women. She could see the curiosity in their eyes, the questions trembling on their lips to know how she'd come to be waiting on the trail alone. *Waiting for Lee.* Telling the story felt too painful. She had claimed that her uncle had taken her along the trail to meet Lee, but then he'd had to go on. When the women's questions became too pointed, Nancy always made an excuse to ease away. *I'm just not like other women. Maybe I never will be.*

It had also been a week since Lee agreed, somewhat reluctantly, to act like her betrothed and keep up the pretense. Nancy despised herself for being so weak she needed to ask him. But what choice did she have? "That Mr. Scott keeps leering at me every chance he gets. Some of those younger fellows whisper... things when they think I can't hear. What else could I do, Charlie?"

And hadn't the other women told her to stay away from the woman named "Hanna?" Nancy surely didn't want to be thought of like her! Although how could you help how a man thought? Like Lee?

Nancy didn't understand Lee at all. While he agreed to pretend to be her betrothed, he wanted to tell Danny it wasn't "for real". Nancy had a problem with that. She had never known many children, but she knew enough to figure they couldn't keep a secret. What was to stop Danny from blurting it out to everyone on the train?

"He might tell someone."

"I can't lie to my brother," Lee insisted. "He knows I didn't ask anyone to wait for me on the trail. He'll wonder why I said that."

"He's just a little boy, he couldn't know everything you do in your life."

"Yes, he could." Those green eyes sized her up and found her wanting in something. Nancy almost shriveled under his intense gaze. "We grew up together in an orphanage. We were pretty much in one another's hip pocket. He knows just about everything about me. I'll tell him he's not to tell."

Although she didn't like the idea, Nancy had to agree that if it became necessary, then Lee could tell Danny. They would try not to appear as a couple around the little ones. If that was the way it had to be, so be it. Nancy sighed.

Even though she hoped she could get to California on her own, Nancy had been glad to see the dust from the wagons coming closer after her wheel broke. Surely, someone was looking out for her. Mama had always believed in God.

Nancy wasn't certain—especially after Mama died and Uncle was so mean. If God was a man, she wanted nothing to do with him. But with the wagon train saving her and Lee coming along to take care of her, maybe it would all be all right. *Maybe there are some men I can trust.*

Maybe Mama had made it to heaven and asked God to send some blessings down her way. Nancy had to admit her heart felt a mite lighter believing it was so. Look at how things worked out. "There I was in a broken-down wagon, one hand on my pistol, afraid I'd be scalped or killed," she rambled to Charlie as he plodded along. "Listening to wolves howl all night long. Staring at those bleached bones..." Nancy shuddered, remembering the bones of cattle beside the trail and a crude gravesite with a wind-worn wooden cross. "Then along came rescue."

The men had repaired her wagon. Lee had hooked up his ox, so she didn't have to wear out Beauty pulling it, and he'd taken it on himself to see to her needs each time they stopped. Pulling the yoke off the ox, going to fetch water or buffalo chips to start a fire, helping her. *Just like a real betrothed might.*

"Hey, Nancy!" Danny ran alongside her wagon, his face reddened by the constant sun beating down. "We're almost to the Platte River and Mr. Trevor says we're going to stop!"

A river! Nancy urged Charlie along a little faster, although as the middle of the train she had other wagons before her. Everyone seemed to catch the excitement. *Water.* All the water they could use. Maybe, she'd take a bath and wash the dust and grime from her hair and clothes. Her clothes. She could wash her clothes... and maybe she could offer to do Lee's and little Danny's too. *Wouldn't that be what a woman would do for the man she loved?*

A wave of guilt washed over her. What would Mr. Morgan think of her feelings for a man she had just met a short week ago? Was she a wicked woman? Had Uncle spoken the truth? *You promised Mr. Morgan you would marry him in your letters. How can you even like Lee Connor?*

"Wagons circle!" Trevor rode his stallion alongside the wagons, his lean, sunburnt face beneath the brown Stetson wearing a smile bigger than Texas. "We're making camp early."

Nancy couldn't wait to step down on solid ground and ease her body from the harsh, unrelenting seat of the wagon. *Water.* Already some of the women and children had run into the shallow river, splashing and pouring it over their heads. As soon as she stopped the wagon, Nancy joined them, yanking off her tight, laced boots and long woolen stockings. Her bare feet felt deliciously free. She danced around in a circle, the bottom of her blue skirt soaking wet and dragging. The river bottom was soft and shifting beneath her bare feet. So cool and refreshing!

"I'm going to wash every stitch I've got," Josephine Evans announced as she scooped up a handful of water to splash across her dusty face. Dirty water sluiced down her cheeks and ran down her bare arms to the sleeves shoved up past her elbows. "Just as soon as I get some of this trail dust off me."

Before they could enjoy the water, there were the inevitable chores of setting up camp. Wagons had to be circled, the livestock—oxen and horses—had to be led to water and picketed in a valley area to graze. The grass appeared sparse and beaten down from wagon trains that had gone before.

But there was still enough for the animals to perk up at the sight of something other than dusty, sunbaked trails. A flock of great blue herons rose and sailed into the cloudless blue of the sky, their cranky squawks announcing disapproval of the human intruders.

The men drew lots to see who would guard the animals first. Nancy couldn't help being a little relieved to hear Mr. Scott's disgruntled voice as he pulled a rifle from his wagon and a plug of tobacco from his pouch. *I'm glad you lost the draw.*

"Men, downriver!" Trevor shouted to be heard over the excited squeals of the children. "Let's let the women stay closer to the wagons."

Most of the other men headed a little downriver to wash off in shifts behind some rocks. The woman took turns holding up sheets so they could bathe modestly and undisturbed. There were children everywhere, splashing, getting washed, playing noisy games as they ran from shore to river.

Once everyone had time to wash off, the women sorted out dirty clothing, gathered washboards and lye soap, and headed back down to the edge of the river. A small group of rocks made a natural working area and the water soon filled with suds and the vigorous up and down of fabric rubbed over washboards. The chattering of women filled the afternoon, like a flock of chittering birds.

Nancy gathered up a wad of her clothing and headed toward the river. On the way, she passed a fresh-scrubbed Lee carrying a little bundle of his own.

"Lee." She felt shy, almost offering. Although she'd washed plenty of Uncle's clothes – underwear and all—this was a stranger. "I'd be happy to wash your and Danny's clothes too."

He blushed. "You don't have to do that. I'm used to washing our things."

"No, now," she insisted, coming close enough so that others couldn't overhear them. "I'll wash them. Folks might think it's strange if I let you do your own wash. Since we're..."

"Oh." He acted as if the thought had never crossed his mind. A flush crossed his face, although it was so tanned from the harsh wind and sun it was hard to tell. He gave her that gap-toothed smile. "Well, I guess you're right." As he handed them to her, their hands accidentally brushed one another.

Nancy felt a tingle but jumped back. *What was that?* She had never felt such a surge of emotion before. What Lee felt she could only guess. He stepped away, unsure and fumbling, "I'm—I'm sorry."

"Don't touch me! I don't want you thinking you can take any liberties with me!" *Men, all men, were such swine! Just like Uncle.* One part of her mind raged, while the other admonished herself, *he didn't mean anything by it.* Suddenly ashamed of the stricken look on his face, she wanted to apologize but didn't know how. *He just brushed my hand; he didn't mean anything by it.*

"Nancy, come with us," Josephine hollered, motioning toward a spot nearby. "We can talk while we wash."

Lee turned and walked away, leaving Nancy with a bundle of clothing in her arms and remorse in her heart. *Why don't I know how men and women talk to one another? What is wrong with me?*

Josephine Evans, a sturdy blue gingham dress tied in a knot at her knees, perched her washboard near a rock. She had a bar of lye soap and a pair of her son's overalls dunked in the river. Barefoot, she stood in water up to her knees and plunked the soiled clothing across the washboard.

Little Mark sat on a rock, pouting, hitting another rock with a stick. "Why can't I go swimming?"

"You don't know how to swim, Mark," Josephine answered patiently, slapping the wet overalls against the rock. "The river's deep out in the middle. You take off your shoes and wade right here. You'll get plenty cooled off."

"I wanna go out with the other boys." He pointed to where some of the older boys had swum to a big rock in the middle of the river. "Now, now, now!" He hit the rock in an annoying way that set Nancy's teeth on edge. "Want to go now!"

"No and I mean it. You can go back to the wagon and pout. You go now, young man." Josephine pointed a stern finger and the little boy stalked off.

As he went, she turned back to Nancy. "That child! But I suppose since his pa died, I'm overprotective of him."

Nancy dunked a pair of little Danny's overalls in the water, wet her own cake of lye soap and lathered them up. The suds turned muddy brown before she dared to ask. "What happened to your...?"

"My husband? He was shot," Josephine rinsed out a pair of her bloomers and laid them over a rock to dry. She picked up a pair of white muslin drawers to rub across the washboard. "His name was Ambrose. He heard about the gold strikes in California, and nothing would do—had to go off. A 'course, he sent money back regularly for Mark and me. But one day he went to the assay office and came back to his claim. A pair of claim jumpers shot him dead."

"I'm sorry." Nancy's heart sped up in a frantic *ta-dump, ta-dump*. Was that the right thing to say when someone told another person something sad? Nancy wasn't rightly sure. Maybe a truly caring person would reach for Josie's hand or quote scripture or something else? *There's so much I don't know—like how to live like other folks do. Even Mama was kind of backward about talking to people because of Uncle. We were like a couple of scaredy chickens, squawking and running for cover when someone tried to be friends. Guess it was just a true miracle I got to be friends at all with Susie.*

Josephine shrugged as she wrung out the drawers and laid them across a rock. "It was a couple of years ago. Mark never met his Pa. We stayed on with my folks for a bit. Then, when Mr. Smith told us he was leading another wagon train out west, I decided now was the time to go. I've got an older son too who went with his Pa. Figured it's time we head on out there. We still own my husband's claim—he built a nice little shanty on it. My older boy, Matthew, keeps it up right fine since those claim jumpers got hung. He's seventeen now. They're all I got now. We lost four between him and Mark."

Nancy thought maybe Josephine would understand her own plight. *She sounds understanding. Wise—almost like Mama—but not as scaredy. Maybe I should tell her...*

Suddenly, a child's scream pierced Nancy's heart like a knife.

Chapter Twelve

Although it could have been any child's voice to Nancy, Josephine's face blanched. "It's Mark! Do you see him?"

Nancy swiveled in a circle, searching for the little boy near the wagons, the water...

"He's in the river!" Josephine screamed, running out into deeper water but stopping when it went past her waist. Her fists hit the water in frustration. Brown water splashed up. "I can't swim! My baby's gonna drown!"

Nancy saw the little boy, arms flailing, trying to reach the older boys near the rock. The boys, busy with a noisy game of their own, didn't notice the younger one. Nancy—who could not swim either—screamed. "Help! Someone help! Mark's going to drown!"

Footsteps hammered past her as a man ran from the shore, dove into the water, and swam with sure-edged strokes toward the boy. As Mark dipped for the third time, sputtering water, the man reached down and yanked him up by an overall strap. The man swam back toward the shore until he could stand where the water wasn't deep. Dripping wet, Lee picked up a limp and sobbing Mark and carried him to set him in Josephine's outstretched arms. Several others had come running up including Freddy and Trevor.

"Boy needs a whipping for scaring us all," Freddy opined, his eyes filled with hate. Nancy had heard him grumble often enough how children didn't belong on a wagon train.

Lee glared at him.

"Looks like he's okay, Miz Evans," Trevor said, "mighty close scare until Lee saved him."

Mark's shuddering sobs kept on, but Josephine grabbed him to the bodice of her gingham dress and held him tight. "Oh, Mark, baby, whatever caused you to do such a wicked thing after Mama told you no?"

"I—I wanted to s-swim like the other boys," Mark gasped right before he spewed water and vomited. "I-I'm sick!"

"You are a naughty, naughty boy—I might have lost you too." Tears pooled in Josephine's' eyes, but she grabbed up a towel to wipe off his tear stained and slimy face. Crooning to him, she rocked him tight in her arms, mother and son both dripping like a leaky pump.

Nancy could only stare at Lee, drenched and wringing the water from his brown, linen shirt. His blond hair streamed into his face; water dripped down his lashes. "He's okay, Mrs. Evans. I think he's scared more than anything. You better get him into dry clothes."

"I will," Josephine answered as she pressed her face to the child's sodden hair. "Then you are going to bed without any supper, young man. You'll not be getting back in that water again."

Mark's wails followed them as Josephine labored up the muddy slope and toward her wagon, the little boy a heavy burden in her arms, as mud squelched beneath her bare feet. Trevor followed along and after a disgusted sneer, Freddy went back to his wagon.

Nancy stared at Lee. *Was there nothing the man couldn't do?* She wanted to say something, but the words caught in her throat.

***

The next day was Sunday, a day of rest. There would be no traveling. Nancy spent the morning folding the clothes she'd washed and laid out to dry the night before. She visited Greta and Eugene for a tin cup of coffee but grew uncomfortable at Greta's questions.

"How long have you known Lee?" Greta wanted to know. "I'm curious where you met him. I met my Eugene at a church social, dancing a jig he was."

"Oh, not long," Nancy mumbled. *I wish I didn't have to pretend.*

"I'd better go see if Lee needs anything," Nancy said as she got up in a hurry, avoiding Greta's penetrating gaze. Smoothing down the lacy ruffles of her Sunday best blue lawn, she tried to look as if she truly wanted to go talk to Lee. *And didn't you dress up specially this morning in hopes he'd notice?*

Greta gave her a smug smile. "Ya, you go and see your young man. I remember how it was."

Sitting by the campfire, Eugene also gave her a knowing smile. For some reason, Nancy's face grew warm as she hurried away. *If they only knew the truth. I'm pledged to Mr. Morgan, not Lee.*

Nancy had no destination in mind, but she decided to walk along the river - just to store up the sight before they had to start on the trail again. Soon, she came upon Lee, Mark, and Danny fishing at the edge of the shore.

This morning, Mark had shown up while Lee helped Nancy start a buffalo chip campfire. The little boy clearly saw Lee as his savior after his scare the day before. He'd brought a present, a smooth rock he'd found at the river's edge. Lee took it like it was a gold nugget.

"Well, now, Mark, I don't think I saw a finer rock. I thank you for the gift of it." Lee told the beaming child. He made a big show of saving it in the pocket of his Sunday pants.

Nancy stood back, watching the patient way Lee helped the little boys put a worm on the end of the hook. Although she couldn't hear what they were saying, both Mark and Danny stared up at Lee with worshipful looks shining on their clean scrubbed faces. He must have made them a fishing "pole" out of long sticks and tied string to a hook.

He's so good with the boys.

She didn't know how long she stood watching, but Nancy couldn't walk away. Lee's kindness seemed to shine like the sun. The way he talked to the boys, put his arm across their shoulders, and gently retied the string each time a hook fell off. *How would it have been to grow up with a father like that?*

What would it be like to really be betrothed to a man so kind and good?

A small stirring in her heart surprised Nancy. The same feeling she'd had the first time she read one of Mr. Morgan's letters. Only this time—the stirring came from looking at Lee.

What does love feel like? How can you truly know? I don't think I love Mr. Morgan. When I think of him, it's more like I think of freedom, not love. Is that wrong?

***

Another week, another endless section of the trail. Lee sighed and ran a damp kerchief across his dirty, sweaty neck. It seemed like months since they'd camped beside the Platte River. He was glad to think tomorrow was another Sunday and a day of rest. It would be good to spend a day out of the wagon and use his legs.

"How long until we get to California, Lee?" Mark asked. "It sure seems like a long way."

"It's going to be a while yet," Lee answered as he smiled down at the little boy. Ever since he'd saved Mark from drowning, the little boy followed him around like a shadow. Thankfully, Danny didn't seem to mind too much. He still spent a lot of his time with Erica and James, helping them around their wagon. Erica felt poorly most days from some strange ailment, so Lee was glad Danny could give her some relief with his antics.

"When Erica feels the worst," James had told him the night before, "that little Danny always gets a chuckle out of her when he talks about those funny tales that happened at the orphanage."

Sure enough wonder what those were. It seemed to Lee each day that they were a million miles further from the Mississippi Orphanage. *I wonder if Mr. Montgomery ever got my letter about Danny?*

"Will we live with you in California, Lee?" Mark asked. "Mama says we are going to live with my brother."

Again, anxious thoughts crowded into his mind. *Where would they go in California?* His friends and neighbors in Natchez had set him off in style – giving him everything he needed to begin the journey. But Lee knew eventually, his supplies were going to run out. He'd have to find a way to support himself and Danny. Hopefully, he could find a town and get work.

"Are you?"

"I might, Mark," Lee answered. "I'm not rightly sure yet."

Lee let Mark's chattering wash over him as they rode the last few miles of the day. Weary to the bone, Lee circled his wagon, unharnessed Cletus, and then went to help Nancy. It would be so good to finally sit down.

"Here's the buffalo chips, Lee," Danny announced, dropping a pile of the hardened mounds of dung he and the other children gathered along the trail. With no wood in sight on these treeless plains, having the chips meant they could build a cook fire at night. At first, the idea of using the chips for cooking turned Lee's stomach. Now, the idea felt like second nature. If a buffalo chip could give him a cup of hot coffee, he welcomed the idea.

"Thanks, Danny. Why don't you and Mark go water the animals? Be sparing with the water though."

They'd stored barrels of water at the Platte—although the joke was that it was too thick to drink. The level of the water in barrels, pots, pans, even unused shoes or boots, was sinking fast. *Sure hope Trevor knows how to find a watering hole before long.*

Lee built a campfire for Nancy—an idea they'd agreed on a few days after Nancy joined the train.

"It doesn't make sense for us to cook supper on different fires," Nancy had whispered one evening when Freddy Scott sent her a curious, smirking glance, "not when we're supposed to be intended for one another."

Nancy turned out to be a fine cook, better than Lee anyway. She also had a good stock of supplies and was generous with the others on the train. Lee knew for a fact that the Richards had run out of coffee a month back.

They used wild chicory to make a bitter tasting brew. When Nancy found out, she always managed to make a tin pot of real coffee and make sure the Richards took it, without hurting their feelings or making it seem like charity. If it meant she had to ask a favor of James – could he water her

ox or repair a hole in the canvas covering of her wagon—
Nancy figured out a way.

*I sure wish I knew her story. Who left her all alone, just like
Charlie, my ox?*

Nancy had just placed a skillet on the fire, filled with slabs
of bacon Lee had sliced, when she looked up and wiped her
hands down the front of a twice-mended calico apron. "Now,
wonder who that is?"

Lee turned to glance down the trail. A single rider, a short
man with an odd, plumed hat, rode toward them on a brown
Saddlebred horse. Standing, Lee went to the wagon and
pulled out his Henry rifle. Other men in the train walked
forward, none of them armed. Not even Trevor. Feeling
embarrassed, Lee put the rifle back in the sling and went to
meet the man. Nancy trailed along behind him. A crowd of
other curious people stood around in a circle, murmuring
among themselves.

"Hello?" The rider called out in a tentative voice, the black
plume of his hat waving in a slight breeze. "I was wondering if
I might join your wagon train, gentlemen."

Trevor glanced at Lee, a perplexed look raising his sandy
eyebrows. "And who might you be?"

"My name is Nick Douglas and I'm afraid I must throw
myself on your mercies."

Chapter Thirteen

"I'm Trevor Smith, the wagon master of this train. This here's Lee Connors, Nancy Fitzgerald..." Trevor introduced the few people who had crowded up to stare at the stranger in a tattered and worn black suit coat with a pair of cavalry blue pants. Lee thought he dressed a lot like the undertaker back in Natchez. His face had a ready smile, although his unusual watery blue eyes seemed peculiar somehow. Like he was looking past them to somewhere else. "Just what is it you want, Mr. Douglas?"

"I'd like to join you if I may, although I must confess, I have nothing to offer in return. I'm the victim of unfortunate circumstances. As you see, I have no wagon, no supplies, no animals other than my horse, Pegasus."

Trevor glanced at Lee who shrugged. Nancy stepped closer to Lee as if she felt unsure or curious. Mark and Danny stood off to the side, staring hard at the odd hat, whispering to one another. "How'd you come to be out here so far from civilization?" Trevor asked, staring hard at the stranger with his brows knotted in thought.

Nick tipped his hat to show a wild mop of dark hair, almost tight curls going every which way. It was hard to tell how old he might be or how young. His face had that pale, delicate pallor of someone not used to outdoor work. *Strange. For someone this far off the trail to be so pale.*

"That is a rather long story, but it commences when my family and I set off from New York to join a wagon train. We found ourselves left behind when an axle broke on the wagon." At this point tears filled his eyes, and his voice shook. "We were set upon one afternoon by renegade soldiers. I'd been out hunting when I heard shots. I went hurrying back to camp to find my wife..." he choked up and almost couldn't go on. "My wife and three children dead. The wagon, oxen, everything gone. They left nothing but the bodies. My surviving son told me who had shot them before he died. He thought Confederate renegades—he said the men wore gray. I don't know. I found myself alone with nothing. I buried my family along the trail."

An odd prickle crawled up Lee's spine. The man sounded truthful, but there was something he was hiding. Lee could sense it. Just like he'd always known when the younger children were lying.

Nancy stepped forward, generous as always. "You can join us for supper. We've got bacon."

The man smiled and put the plumed hat back on his head. "I thank you kindly, ma'am. However, I've yet to hear Mr. Smith's answer to whether I can join your train."

Trevor glanced at Lee, clearly worried. Lee understood. Trevor had charge of all these people. Back at the orphanage, Lee had often felt the pressure of taking care of his orphaned brothers and sisters. He knew firsthand how terrible he felt when one of them was sick or hurt.

How much more Trevor must feel this now? While Tad was scouting, Trevor oversaw keeping everyone safe, together and hopefully alive. If taking care of the orphans had been a pebble-sized responsibility for Lee, he knew Trevor's responsibility was the size of a mountain.

Tad Marshall was somewhere up ahead scouting their route. An experienced trapper and hunter, Mr. Marshall rarely stayed with the train. Lee could remember having only one conversation with the man in the days since they'd left Independence. Any decisions would be left to Trevor unless he asked them all to take a vote. "Excuse me a minute, sir. Lee..." he motioned Lee off to the side. "What do you think,

Lee?" Trevor whispered with a worried glance back at the stranger. "If I let someone unknown join us, a person without food or supplies, it could hinder the rest of us from reaching California."

"That's true enough," Lee glanced back at the man, sitting silently in the saddle, the silly plume of his hat the only thing brave about him. There was something appealing about the man and if he had truly lost everything he owned, it was only decent to help him. "It wouldn't feel right to leave him out here alone."

"You may be the only one who thinks that," Trevor said as he glanced back at the people crowding around, murmuring. "From the looks of some of those faces, they can see trouble ahead if we let him join us. What if he's some type of thief, come to do us harm? You're young yet, you haven't met all the evil I have out here on the trail."

"He can travel with me and Danny, Trevor," Lee said, honored to have Trevor ask for his opinion. *He and Thomas are a lot alike. I'm glad to call him my friend now, too.* "If you're agreeable to letting him join on. We'll share what we have, and I can keep an eye on him. He looks harmless enough. He doesn't even have a gun, far as I can see."

"I can share too," Nancy interrupted. Before he could stop himself, Lee reached out to grasp Nancy's hand. He intended to mean it as a "thank you" but found himself oddly moved by her warm hand in his. Just as quickly, remembering her anger once before, he dropped it. To his relief, Nancy gave him a timid smile as if she hadn't minded at all. "I'm willing. You all took me in when I was alone. I'd like to return the favor to someone else."

"Well," Trevor appeared to think it over. "If you'll take charge of him and share your supplies, I guess that's settled.

But, he's your responsibility, Lee. If others complain, you might be forced to make some hard decisions."

"I understand."

"Do you? If Nick slows you down or uses the supplies you need, you may be on your own. Others have been stopped in the Rockies before without provisions. You've surely heard of the Donner Party. Times could get rough."

Lee shuddered, remembering stories he'd read about the ill-fated Donner Party. Still, Lee couldn't just abandon the man. He walked back up to the man, smiling to himself over that silly plumed hat. "You're welcome to ride with me, Mr. Douglas. With my brother and me."

I just hope I'm making the right decision.

Thankfully, Freddy Scott was not in the crowd of curious onlookers. A few scattered people murmured among themselves and didn't seem to be in favor of allowing Nick to come along.

"He better not slow us down," a voice grumbled. Spence, one of the "outlaws."

"Asking for trouble," another answered. "Don't know anything about him at all."

Although James Richards nodded his approval, several other men, including the rest of the "outlaws", were scowling at this new development.

I hope I haven't endangered everyone.

***

Another day, another mile, another agonizing minute of choking dust. Lee found himself half dozing on the hard wagon seat, coming to with a jolt when the wheels hit a rut.

As he drove Cletus, Lee worried. The Belgian didn't appear as spry as he had when they'd started out. Even a sturdy horse got tired of pulling a 1000-pound wagon along behind day after day.

"You might consider selling the horse and buying a mule or oxen when we reach Fort Laramie," Trevor had suggested last night at supper. "You'd do better with something more reliable once we reach the Rockies. The mountains can be rough, and horses aren't the best for pulling wagons. You think on it."

Lee had thought of nothing else since. Although he disliked the idea of parting from Cletus, he had to do whatever was necessary to ensure his and Danny's safety. Nancy's too, and now, Mr. Douglas. *I've sure enough got more responsibilities than I bargained for when I left Mississippi. Almost like taking care of a bunch of orphans again.*

A sudden gust of wind tugged Lee's wide-brimmed hat. His eyes watered from the hard, piercing dirt as a cloud of brown grit whirled before him. The dirt was so thick, he could only dimly see the back of Nancy's wagon before his. *What in tarnation?*

Danny ran up alongside the wagon, struggling to stay on his feet. His small hat blew off his head and he lost the battle to grab it. In seconds, it was lost in the twirling, whirling cloud.

"Lee! Mr. Smith said a storm's coming. We need to make camp and shelter now!"

"Danny! Get up here!" Lee yanked Cletus to a halt as Danny scrambled into the wagon. Through the blinding dust, a jagged fork of lightning pierced the sky like a rattlesnake's fangs. Angry rumbles of thunder echoed across the plains announcing a fearsome storm to follow.

Mr. Douglas, who'd been riding in the wagon bed, peered through the canvas opening. "What's happening?" Although he often rode Pegasus and followed Lee's wagon, today the horse appeared to have a slight limp. Hopefully, a day without a rider would heal him to travel on. "Why are we stopping?"

Now what kind of fool question is that? Lee wondered. *Anybody can see. Or hear.*

"It's a storm." Bits of grit and sand sailed into Lee's mouth. Spitting, he pressed his lips tight. The wind showed no mercy in pricking his face with hard chips of gravel and dead plants spiked as needles. Lee tasted blood as something cut his lip.

"I can't hardly see," Danny moaned, then coughed on the choking dust. "It's blowing too hard."

"Pull your kerchief up to your eyes," Lee advised, pulling up his own red kerchief until it covered his mouth and nose. By tugging his wide-brimmed hat as far down over his ears as possible, he managed to squint into the dusty, brown whirlwind before him. "Get in back. Stay in the wagon, Danny! Don't you dare get out."

"Wagons circle! Wagons circle! Shelter from the storm!" The words passed up and down the train as everyone managed to circle the wagons, untie the livestock, and pen them in the space between the wagons. Working for the good of all, everyone bent to a task, helping unyoke oxen or teams, tying down the canvas coverings that flapped in the fierce, unrelenting tugging wind.

Pucker ropes at each end of the canvas pulled the covers tight in hopes of keeping out the dust and grit. Nancy, green skirts whipping in the wind, struggled to yank the canvas taut on her wagon. Her blue eyes caught Lee's glance for an instant, but she didn't ask for help or appear frightened.

Lee, intent on unharnessing Charlie, Beauty, and Nick's Pegasus, glanced up to see even Freddy and the "outlaws" hard at work preparing to shelter from the storm. They lent a hand to Mrs. Evans and another family who had several small children.

"Nick, come help me!" Lee hollered into the blowing wind, tugging a length of rope out of the wagon bed. The fierce shrieks of wind screamed over his words. "I'm going to tie a picket rope between my wagon and Nancy's to keep the horses safe." Lee tied one end of the hemp to the curved wooden support and handed the other end of the stout rope to Nick. The man bent into the wind and stumbled toward Nancy's wagon. "Make sure it's tight!"

Lee had no way to know if Nick heard. The wind had reached a high pitch, stealing words and breath. Beauty and Cletus both yanked at his tight grip on the harness, snorting and high-stepping enough to jerk his arms half out of their sockets. Beauty's eyes rolled in fear and Cletus snorted his disapproval. Pegasus spooked but Lee managed to get the Saddlebred under control. "Easy, now, easy." Lee tried to calm the horses with little success. It took effort to pull off the harness and reins, and the muscles in his arms screamed in agony. Charlie didn't seem as frightened although his brown eyes rolled, and he stomped a hoof hard on the ground.

Nancy came up, wind tossing the ends of her brown curls and tugging at the scarf she held tight over her head and face. Only a slit for her watering eyes, squinting against the grit, showed through.

"I'm going to help Greta and Eugene!" She shouted to be heard. "If you think the horses are tied up tight."

"Stay beside the wagons! Hold tight!" Lee yelled back, the wind taking that second to shriek like a howling banshee. Rain pattered down, soaking him in an instant. It was cold rain too, drenching his brown linen shirt. As much as he wanted to help Nancy, he had to keep his mind on the task at hand. *If the animals get away...*

"Nick, what are you–"

The fearsome wind had jerked the rope from Nick's hand. One end of the rope blew like a snake back and forth, playing tug of war with the knot tied to the wagon. Lee stared, astounded, as Nick reached out a fumbling, searching hand, feeling thin air as he tried to find the rope. The rope sailed within inches of his hand, but Nick did not grasp it. Did not see it. *Could* not see it.

He's blind!

Chapter Fourteen

The knowledge came as chilling as the cold rain that pelted Lee's blond hair. *How could he be blind?* But there could be no other explanation for a man not to see a rope dangling inches before his face.

Stepping forward, Lee grabbed the end of the rope, Nick's hand, and placed the rope in the man's palm. "It's here. Can you tie a proper knot, so the horses don't run off?"

"Yes," Nick mumbled in a humble voice, "I can do that. Lee... I..."

"Do it and get back in the wagon with Danny." Lee wanted no explanations just then. Could listen to no reasons. *Blind! What have I done taking him on?* "I need to check on the others."

He didn't wait to see if Nick answered or obeyed. Stumbling in the pelting rain, Lee kept the secret he'd just learned tight in his mind. Blind! How had he even found the train without sight? And what part of his story was true? Any of it?

He shoved the questions away as he stumbled in the deepening mud as rain pelted his face, water cascaded down his cheeks. Holding onto the wagon wheels, he pulled himself down the row until he found McGregor's wagon. His boots squelched in the mud as he slipped for a hold.

"Nancy! Are you all right? Greta? Eugene?"

"Yes, we're fine," Nancy called out as he stopped by the back of the wagon, canvas top snapping in the wind but holding taut. Nancy peered through the puckered opening slit, brown curls damp on her forehead. "We've got Josephine and Mark too! It's crowded in here but we're fine."

"Aye," Eugene called out, "get back to your own wagon, son. We're fine to weather the storm. Greta's got dried fruit and hardtack to tide us over. We've blankets a'plenty. No need to worry about us."

Lee needed no other encouragement. Thunder boomed overhead and shook the very earth he stood on. The horses whinnied in fear, tugging hard at the picket lines. Still, it looked as if Nick had tied the rope taut. Lee checked to make sure, his hand tugging at the tight knot.

Reassured the horses were secure, Lee gave them each a pat, sorry he couldn't feed them or let them graze. Hopefully, the storm would not last too long. Any grain he put out would be sodden in the cold, drenching rain. Again, jagged forks of lightning lit up the darkness overtaking the day. It would soon be as black as pitch.

Lee shivered and climbed up into the wagon to join Danny and Nick in what might be a long, blustery night.

He was soaked to the skin. There seemed no point in trying to find dry clothes for himself. The canvas leaked in places and Lee knew he might have to go back outside at any time to check on the animals. Wet clothes were uncomfortable, but he'd been in worse discomfort before. Water squelched inside his boots, his woolen socks wet and miserable. As hot as he'd been earlier in the day, he'd trade the penetrating cold and rain for just a few degrees of the sunbaked heat.

"I-I'm cold, Lee," Danny shivered inside the wagon, dripping wet.

"Danny! I thought I told you to stay inside?"

"I'm sorry, I had to go outside. The McGregor's cow, Buttercup, broke loose and I had to save her."

Danny and his love of animals! Lee couldn't be annoyed. "Well, I guess there wasn't anything else you could do. Is she all right now?"

Teeth chattering, Danny nodded. "I t-t-tied her to Nancy's wagon wheel."

Kneeling beside their trunk, a shovel poking him in the back, Lee pulled out a dry nightshirt for Danny and towels. "Here, you get out of those wet clothes and dry off." Shivering, Danny shucked off dripping overalls and a flannel shirt. Lee dried off his brother, then his own face and wet hair. The wet clothes would have to lie in a damp pile on top of the cornmeal barrel.

Lee unfolded their stack of woolen blankets and wrapped one around the little boy.

"I-I'm scared, L-lee." Danny shivered on a pallet Lee made in the crowded middle of the wagon. There wasn't much of a spare inch to sit down, much less sleep.

With all their supplies packed tight, there was only a narrow path through the barrels, cooking gear, clothes, and tools. Nick, as if knowing Lee did not want to discuss what had happened, sat near the opening to the wagon seat, the canvas covering pulled tight against the rain's steady assault. The man hunched over, a woolen blanket covering his wet clothes, his sightless eyes closed.

Blind! How is it possible?

"It's just a storm, Danny. We been through lots worse at the orphanage," he tried to reassure the little boy. Rummaging through one of the food barrels, he pulled out a cloth sack of dried apple slices. "Let's eat supper. It's not much, but we can fill our bellies and try to get some sleep. Bet this storm blows over before morning."

Lee passed Danny apple slices and chewed a few himself, although the food did little to stop the rumbling in his stomach. *A hot cup of coffee would taste right fine about now.*

The rain made a peculiar pattering sound on the canvas over their heads. Inside the wagon, Danny sniffled but soon fell asleep. Lee made sure to cover him well and sat down beside him. Although he didn't think he'd fall asleep, as damp and uncomfortable as he felt, Lee started awake at a loud noise.

"Danny?" he whispered.

Hearing the steady breathing of the little boy, and an answering rumble from the corner where Nick slept, Lee sat straighter, stiff and damp. Outside the rain continued to pelt the wagon cover and loud booms of thunder echoed across the plains. He knew he'd heard a sound. A voice—no, a shout.

"Get out!"

The hateful words carried through the sounds of the wind and rain. Lee had no idea who had shouted them or why. Easing around Danny, he climbed out of the wagon into the rain-driven night.

Once outside, he could hear the voices, quarreling, a woman's pitiful tears and entreaties. "Don't do this," she cried, "It's storming out here. Freddy, let me back inside! I can't even pitch my tent in this storm."

Freddy's wagon then. It must be Hanna. He threw her out into the rain.

Lee had seen Hanna enter Freddy's wagon a few different nights. Although Trevor had confided he didn't like it, there was nothing he could do short of ordering Freddy to leave them. Some of the other men in the train, such as the "outlaws" used bawdy slurs to talk about Hanna. Even though Lee knew he was not totally innocent about what happened between men and women, he'd never heard most of the names the men called Hanna. Still, she was a woman and she'd been turned out into the storm.

What should I do? What would Thomas do?

Maybe Hanna would find another wagon to share? *Who? Where? She can't pitch her tent in this downpour.*

Lee sighed. *What would Thomas do? Thomas would come to her rescue.*

"Hanna?"

"What? Who?" Hanna stopped, tugging a sodden shawl around her head and shoulders. The dress she wore had been ripped near the bodice and Lee had to keep his eyes away from a lacy edge of lady's unmentionables peeking through the hole. His face flamed despite the raindrops dripping across his cheeks. "Oh, Lee, I guess you heard. I'm without a bedroom for the night."

Water dripped from the ends of her wild mop of hair, something dark—*paint?*—smeared around her eyes and cheeks. Clearly, some of the wetness on her face was tears, not rain. As she stumbled through the mud—barefoot, Lee noticed—she gulped and choked on a sob.

"Miss Hanna..." Was she *Miss*? Lee realized he didn't know. He thought of Nancy's empty wagon but knew he didn't dare offer that as a choice. Nancy, like all the women on the train, had made it clear she preferred not to associate with Hanna any more than necessary. "I can't offer you room in my wagon. We're crammed as it is, but I can put up my waterproof poncho and fix you a place under the wagon. I've got warm blankets. You'd be out of the rain and somewhat dry."

Although what will Nancy say?

Although, considering the torrents of rain falling from the gunmetal gray sky, dry might be a chancy thing for the night. Lee couldn't see Hanna's face too well in the darkness, but another sob caught in her throat before she answered in a halting voice, smelling of the sour odor of whiskey. "T-thank you, Lee. I think I might take you up on that. Since I've nowhere else to go."

It took a little time to climb back in his wagon and pull out the waterproof tent, blankets, and dry towels without waking Danny or Nick. Once back outside, Lee hurried to fix a spot under the wagon, thankful the ground appeared drier than the rest of the world just then. He spread the waterproof poncho and blankets, and offered Hanna towels he'd wrapped in oil cloth to keep dry. "I've got some dried apple slices," he said as she half crawled, half stumbled into her temporary bedroom, "if you're hungry."

Hanna gave a funny laugh. "No, but thank you anyway. You better try to get dried off yourself. It feels like it's going to rain forever and drown us all. Maybe it would be better that way. If we all died right here."

There was no answer Lee could find for that. He left her and climbed back into the wagon, dripping again, and tried to settle himself for a cold, damp night's sleep. Whatever was left of the night. It felt near dawn. He didn't think he'd drifted off, but again a shout woke him.

Fuzzy-headed, Lee jerked awake.

"Fire! Fire!"

Chapter Sixteen

"Fire! Everyone Out! Help!" Trevor's voice shouted orders as he ran past Lee's wagon, the words echoing around the circled wagons. "Help, everyone, we need everyone!"

Other voices took up the cry, shouting, calling. "Fire! Fire!"

Stumbling, still half asleep and bleary-eyed, Lee stepped over Danny as the little boy sat up, "What's wrong? What's happening?" His voice trembled as he pulled the blanket around his shoulders. "Why are people hollering?"

"Fire—something's on fire." Lee spoke in a hurry as he made his way over the barrels and toolbox to climb out of the wagon. He barked his shin on the edge of the clothes truck but didn't stop to rub the sore. "You stay inside for now," he told Danny, surprised at how calm his voice sounded to his own ears. At the end of the wagon, he saw Nick stirring but making no move to follow. "Nick, keep Danny in here."

What can a blind man do anyway?

The rain had finally ended, but a brilliant light surrounded a wagon down the train. Fierce orange flames sparked and crackled in the night, sending up cinders as it ate up the dry goods inside the wagon—ready-made clothing, towels, fabric and those pricey matches. Still wet, the canvas sent out mostly dark smoke, creating a smudge of fire to choke Lee as he ran toward the scene.

Freddy's wagon!

"Hurry," Trevor shouted as the "outlaws" rushed up, some of them barefoot and one with only his long red, flannel underwear on. "We need to pull this wagon away from the others! He's carrying gunpowder in there!"

118

Thankfully, the men, with Spence in the lead, grabbed the tongue of the wagon and pulled it out of the circle. Other members of the train, most half-dressed in night clothes and hastily pulled on pants, rushed to help. The fully loaded wagon was too heavy to move far, but to Lee's relief he saw they'd managed to get it away from the other wagons nearby. Far enough away to avoid sparks hitting the other wagons if the gunpowder exploded.

A couple of the women, Nancy and Josephine included, dunked towels in their buckets of water to douse sparks that might land on wagons nearby. The slap, slap of the towels hit other wagon beds as they kept a vigilant watch. Even with the dampness, a stray spark could wreak havoc if it landed inside someone's stored goods.

Lee had known even flour to explode given the right amount of heat. *If the gunpowder or kerosene went...* The canvas covering of Freddy's wagon was probably waterproofed with paraffin like most of the others. Once it got warm enough, it would burn too.

James Richards, half-dressed in a pair of inside-out broadcloth trousers and suspenders, caught Lee by the arm as he hurried up. "Help me get these animals moved away. They're spooked by this smoke! We've got enough trouble without a stampede."

"What happened? How did it start?" Lee asked as he hurried to James' side.

Muscles straining in his dark arms, James snagged a picket rope and tossed the loop to Lee, fighting against the ox's strength. "Not sure," he panted, "someone said Freddy dropped a cigar and the fire started inside the wagon before he realized. Grab this rope!"

Lee grabbed the length of rope James had tied around an ox's neck and led the animal into the center of the circled wagons. It wasn't an easy task; the animal bellowed and refused to budge at first. James hurried along behind the other ox and Freddy's horse, the high-spirited Morgan whinnying in fear, dark eyes rolling as it shied away from the flames.

James had to grab up some woman's dish towel to toss over the horse's eyes to lead him to safety. Some of the other horses were spooked by the crackling fire, and the milk cows the McGregor's had brought along bellowed in fear. It took strong arms and stamina for Lee to get the ox far enough to hand over the rope to Eugene McGregor who stood beside his wagon, shivering in a patchwork quilt.

"Where's Freddy?" he asked as he tied the ox to a picket rope by his own wagon. "Is he safe?"

"I don't know…" Lee hurried back to the wagon. The fire had now eaten into the wood on one side of the wagon, the canvas totally consumed and dropping in black, melting chunks onto all the goods stored in the wagon. *I knew that paraffin would ignite.* As Lee watched, a barrel of shovel handles began to burn like Roman candles lighting the night. The heat from the wagon prickled Lee's face and took his breath away.

"Help me," Freddy shouted, brushing off cinders and not seeming to notice the danger. Scurrying inside the burning wagon, he picked up boxes and crates to toss out into outstretched hands. Red-faced and struggling, he tripped in the narrow confines of the burning wagon. "Help me get my merchandise out!"

Some of the men were able to grab things Freddy tossed, smaller boxes and crates. Two of the "outlaws" went so far as to jump inside and haul out a barrel of flour and another of corn meal. Brushing off sparks that landed in their hair and bare shoulders, they made a hasty retreat. After that, they tried to force Freddy to abandon the wagon.

"Come out of there!" Spence hollered, "You can't save it all. If flames hit that gunpowder or kerosene..."

The man who had taken Hanna into a tent in Independence—Virgil, Lee knew now—wiped rain and soot from his flushed face, hopped back into the wagon and grabbed Freddy's arm. "Get out! You're gonna burn!"

The solid hickory wagon tongue burst into flames, the warmth of the fire spreading out in sudden intensity. Flames shot up—orange, deep yellow and almost black in the first faint bluish tint of dawn. Lee stumbled back as the wagon seat caught fire and burned like a runaway wildfire.

The fire's heat soared out like a blast from a farrier's forge. Hard to believe with everything soaked hours earlier – but the fire inside the wagon had dried the wood to ignite. People didn't realize, but Lee had worked with enough wood to know, sometimes wet wood burned faster and hotter than unseasoned, green wood.

"Freddy, get out, now!" Trevor shouted at the man. 'Nothing's worth your life!"

"I've got to save my merchandise," Freddy shouted back as an ember dropped to the shoulder of his long underwear and burnt a hole. He brushed it off without thought, his eyes wild in his soot-streaked face. Burning embers dropped on his bald head, but Freddie acted as if he didn't even feel the blisters they raised on his scalp. "Help me! Help me! I can't lose everything!"

"That durn fool!" Trevor shouted and jumped to the back of the wagon bed, pushing aside a barrel of smoldering foodstuffs to take a firm hold of Freddy's shoulder. "Lee! Help me get him out of here! You've got to get out now!"

Lee didn't want to jump into the burning wagon, but he climbed on one of the wagon wheels and reached out for Freddy's arm as Trevor stumbled over a stack of blankets. Freddy fought like a wildcat, yanking Lee over into the wagon bed, screaming, "Let me go! I need to save my things! My strongbox! My money!"

"Lee!" Trevor hollered the one word, but by then Lee had gotten a better grip on Freddy's arms and tugged toward the only part of the wagon still solid. The wood beneath his hand was so hot, it burnt his palm.

"Ow! Help, someone!"

James was there with Spence to help Lee haul the sutler out. Between the three of them, they half-dragged, half-carried Freddy to a grassy spot a few feet away from the wagon. Just in time.

With no warning, the intense heat hit a can of kerosene and it exploded. The loud shatter split the night louder than any rumble of thunder. Burning chunks of wood sailed into the sky and thudded back to earth with their dangerous sparks. Again, Nancy and the other women used wet towels to slap, slap, slap at the sparks showered on innocent wagons. A second later the flames hit the gunpowder and the explosion rocked the earth.

What if I'd been in there? Despite the powerful heat, Lee shook as if he had the worst chill he'd ever had. His legs refused to hold him, and he slumped to the ground. *What would happen to Danny if I died?*

Everyone jumped back and one of the women screamed. Mark Evans' fretful cries could be heard as they all stood in the growing dawn, watching the wagon burn. The whole wagon bed, made from solid hickory, burnt like the biggest campfire they'd ever seen.

The flames licked their way through the wood and the boxes, barrels, crates and hanging ready-made clothes Freddy had for sale. Lee had never watched a fire consume things, outlining each shape before it dropped into ash and soot. The heat was so intense they kept stepping back, away from the blaze.

There go barrels of flour, cornmeal, beans, and I don't know what all. All those things Freddy wanted to sell for three times the price.

As if it were a living thing, the fire roared and screamed, crackling with glee as it ate through all the goods Freddy had hoped to sell on the trail. He'd been driving a six yoke Conestoga wagon—heavy, cumbersome and loaded to the canvas covering. Just like that—gone.

It was probably wrong to think of someone's misfortune and be glad, but Lee thought of a Bible verse Mr. Montgomery used to recite. "Pride goeth before a fall." *Somehow, it fits.*

Everyone stood watching the fire consume Freddy's wagon as the drizzle ebbed and stopped. A few stray raindrops sizzled on the dying embers and the wagon crumbled into burning chunks of wood, the steel rims of the wagon wheels twisting from the intense heat. By dawn, all that was left were charred hunks of wood, twisted metal and piles of bolts or screws, a stench of burnt flour and sugar, and an odd popping sound as some of the tin cans burst.

Almost wearier than he'd ever been, Lee turned away from the fire to check on Nancy and saw her at the very edge of the group. She still wore the dark green dress she'd had on earlier today, her eyes red-rimmed and haunted. Brown curls straggled down her neck as she wiped a sooty hand across her cheek. She glanced at Lee then quickly turned away. He sighed and trudged back to the wagon to check on Danny.

At least none of us got hurt.

***

A cigar. Just a few embers from a dropped cigar. Like a man couldn't have a few pleasures without falling asleep to disaster.

"I'm sorry, Freddy," Trevor said that morning as they looked at the smoldering ruins of his dream. "Hanna said she saw flames and smoke coming from inside your wagon and raised the alarm, but by then some of the dry goods inside had caught fire. Hard to believe it burned so fast with all the rain we had, but I guess once it hit the gunpowder... there was no chance to save anything. I guess it's good she woke me, or you might be dead now. You have to count your blessings you made it out alive."

Blessings! Ha!

Freddy spit on the ground and cursed under his breath, so angry he thought his head might explode from the hatred churning inside. Clenching his hands, he ground the nails into his palms until they bled.

Blessings! More like curses!

He glared at the remains of his wagon and the lost profits he'd hoped to have when he reached California. He'd been on the trail many times before and knew how desperate people got once they reached the Rockies or the desert. When it came to paying him a week's wages for one small item or killing an ox for food, most of the travelers had been willing to fill his coin purse. He felt no shame in providing what others were too foolish or unwise to pack. Now, thanks to *them*, he was ruined.

They could have helped me! If Trevor Smith had told the other men to help empty the wagon, we could have done it before everything burned. And that Lee Connors, I know he took Hanna in last night. If he hadn't jumped in to be a hero, I'd have let her back in after a while. We'd have seen the fire earlier, maybe in time to save more. I wouldn't have left her outside all night—just long enough to show her who's in charge. I wouldn't have drunk all that whiskey and fallen asleep with a lit cigar ...

Freddy stared at the pitiful pile of goods he'd managed to save. One barrel of flour and one of cornmeal. A box of ready-made boots and woolen stockings. An almost useless box of two-penny nails. The grease bucket he kept to ensure his wagon wheels were oiled. Wagon wheels now burned into charred hunks of wood and twisted metal rims.

There was one crate of whiskey he'd saved. That could be useful, but not too much profit. A few other small items that could turn a profit eventually, but not enough to pay for all the trouble of coming along on this trip. All the tobacco, foodstuffs, patent medicines, water buckets...Freddy couldn't even begin to inventory his complete stock. The loss was too enormous to comprehend. Just thinking of the enormity of it made his head throb.

I'm ruined. My strongbox is gone, my clothes, my Colt. He grimaced at the misshapen trousers and too-tight linen shirt one of the other men had loaned him this morning. Thankfully, he'd been wearing his own boots when the fire began. He knew from his previous travels they'd come to a fort soon—Fort Laramie. If he still had the strongbox, he could have bought more supplies, restocked his wagon.

But what would he do now? With no money to purchase more or even to return back to Arkansas, he was penniless. He still had the oxen; perhaps they could be sold or traded. Without a wagon or merchandise, he had no use for oxen.

Staring at his worldly goods in the smoldering ruins of his wagon, Freddy made a vow. *They won't get away with this. If it's the last thing I do, Trevor Smith and Lee Collins will pay me for my loss.*

Although he had no idea how he'd manage to make Trevor Smith pay, his eyes took on a wicked gleam when he thought of Lee Collins and his "betrothed." Maybe soon Lee would understand how it felt to lose the most precious thing he owned.

Chapter Seventeen

"Lee, how come we can't move any faster?" Danny wanted to know on the third day after Freddy's wagon had caught fire. "It's not raining all that bad. Just a sprinkle."

Sitting on the wagon seat, hands on the reins, Lee sighed as another cold finger of rain slid down the back of his collar. Not that the rest of him wasn't as wet, but those little slithers of rain were like an insult to injury. All morning long a steady drizzle came down, until everything dripped—people, animals, and wagons. If they'd managed to drive two miles, Lee would be surprised. "It's not safe to move so fast in the rain, Danny. I guess we probably shouldn't be trying to move ahead at all, but Trevor says we have to push on whenever we can. It's still a long way to California."

"I'm dripping all over," Danny grumbled, "and it's too hard to walk alongside the wagon in all that mud. An' how we gonna start a fire if we can't gather any buffalo chips? I sure do wish we could have some hot soup. Mud, mud, mud!"

The mud made it harder for the animals to pull the wagons too. Earlier that morning, after another series of storms like the one when Freddy's wagon burnt, Trevor had made the decision to start out. The morning had begun fair and cloudy, but dry. About ten, the sky opened and drenched them all. Again.

I never knew there was this much rain in the clouds. Guess if the Almighty wants to drown us, He's off to a good start.

"We'll try to travel a few miles further," Trevor decided. "We'll see how far we get by noon."

It had been a useless trial as far as Lee was concerned. The wagon wheels were mired in mud, the oxen or horses couldn't pull hard or fast enough to make progress. Cursing filled the air as the men driving the wagons had to get out and pull the tired animals forward by the yoke, their legs knee-deep in thick, unforgiving mud.

Twice, Nancy's wagon wheels had sunk so deep it was necessary for several men to put their shoulders to the iron-tired wheels and push her out of ruts. Her wagon wasn't the only one to suffer such a fate. Others in the train mired down every few feet. Sweating, grunting, soaking, the men accepted the chore and went to help whoever was in need.

Trevor rode up on his black stallion. Covered in his rain poncho, his dark Stetson dripping and soggy, he reined in beside Lee. "We're going to make camp and just sit tight until it quits. This is too hard on everyone. We're going to have to lighten the loads too. Can you help the McGregors get settled? Eugene's in a bad way so I've got Freddy driving his wagon. Where's Nick?"

"Surely," Lee promised. "I've noticed Eugene's been coughing a lot since that last storm. Nick thought he'd ride with Nancy a spell and help her," he lied, aware of Danny beside him. Truthfully, he had suggested Nancy let Nick ride with her awhile to lighten the load on his wagon. He wasn't ready to confess to anyone, least of all Trevor or Nancy, about Nick's infirmity.

I've got to find time to talk to Nick!

Trevor tipped a salute to the edge of his soppy hat and rode on down to tell the rest of the wagons to make camp.

Although Nancy hadn't questioned it, her cornflower blue eyes studied Nick as if she knew there must be more to the suggestion. Lee had seen other eyes studying him, probably wondering why Nick didn't help shove wagons out of mud or drive Nancy's wagon. *Like a blind man can do anything?*

The knowledge hidden in his mind about Nick's blindness weighed like an enormous burden. Lee knew there needed to come a time when he talked to Nick and demanded clear answers, but there was no privacy. The storm, then Freddy's wagon burning, the agony of waiting out the storms that followed.

Everyone's fears were about reaching California in time, before snow blocked the Rockies. Lee had heard more than a few nervous whispers about the Donner party. Each day they lost without traveling weighed as heavy as a millstone.

"I'm glad we're stopping," Danny said, "but I wish we could build a fire when we do. I'm as wet as a Mississippi mud rat."

"What's a Mississippi mud rat?"

"Not sure." Danny shrugged. "That's always what Old Sam used to say when any of us boys got all wet and dirty. I sure do miss him, don't you, Lee? And everybody back home?"

Unexpected tears moistened Lee's eyes. *I sure do.* "Oh, sometimes, but we came out here to have adventures. When we get to California, we'll have a fine ranch. Maybe one day, we can invite some of the other boys to come visit us. I read in the newspaper one day there's going to be a railroad train that comes clear across the continent. All the way from the Atlantic Ocean to the Pacific Ocean. They could ride on that."

"Sure wish it was built now," Danny grumbled, sniffing, and wiping raindrops from his eyelashes. "I'd sure rather ride a railroad train than be out here. When we stop, can I go see what Mark is doing?"

"After we set up camp. You got chores."

"How come Nick never has to do chores?"

Lee shifted on the seat as he set the brake. "We'll talk about it some other time. Nick's got a... well, a problem. It makes it hard for him to do the same things we do."

"What kind of a problem?"

"We'll talk about it some other time. When you finish chores, you can find Mark. Might be I can find some licorice as a treat."

"Licorice! Oh, boy!"

It was easy to turn Danny's mind away from Nick, but what about the others on the train? Eventually, Lee knew the truth would come out. It was a moment he dreaded.

As soon as he'd unharnessed Cletus and helped Nancy unhitch, Lee hurried to the McGregors' wagon. Freddy might have driven them into camp, but he didn't lift a finger to help make camp. He'd offered another man the use of his oxen in return for food until they reached the fort. After he braked the McGregor's wagon, Freddie hurried off.

Maybe he's hoping Hanna will cook something for him. To Lee's surprise, Hanna didn't appear to be angry at Freddy tossing her out the night of the fire. The next morning she'd been hanging all over him, fixing him breakfast from her supplies and fawning over him while he glared at her.

To each his own.

After taking care of the McGregor's oxen and cows, Lee climbed into the wagon bed, careful not to bump his head on the oil lamp Greta had hung from the overhead bow of the wagon. To his dismay, he found Eugene lying inside the wagon on a pallet of quilts, shivering beneath another pile. Greta sat nearby, perched on top of a barrel of lard, her gnarled fingers twisting a once-white handkerchief. A few days before, she'd been forced to leave her cherished rocking chair beside the trail. "Oh, Lee, thank you so much for looking out for us!"

Eugene gave a rattly cough and couldn't seem to stop. "T-th..." he couldn't manage the word without his body shaking from the cough. Flush-faced, his eyes red and watering, the old man trembled.

"I wish we could build a fire! He needs warm broth," Greta fretted, "not hardtack and dried fruit. When will this dratted rain stop?"

"Don't you worry about that," Lee tried to reassure her, despite the dread he felt at seeing Eugene in such a condition, "I'm going to put up a waterproof and build a fire. I had Danny hold back some buffalo chips, so we'd have something to use." Lee also didn't mention he planned to take an ax and chop up the wooden trunk they used for clothing. Firewood meant more now than a trunk. Eugene's health came first and that meant getting a good, hot meal into him so he could get well. A trunk could be rebuilt; Eugene couldn't.

"Bless you, bless you." Greta clapped her hands, a flicker of a smile on her rosy cheeks. "Now you be sure to get the pail from under the wagon. I'm not sure there's butter with the way we been travelin', but you give it to Nancy if there is. She can have some of my white flour too and mix up some biscuits in my Dutch oven."

James Richards had taken over milking Buttercup and Sweet Pea in the mornings for a share of the fresh milk for Erica since Eugene had fallen ill. Lee didn't know if they'd traveled long enough today for butter to set, but Nancy would be happy with whatever he gave her.

Lee nodded and started off to build the fire. He ran into Nancy just outside the wagon, carrying a small basket with herbs and patent medicines. A frown marred her pale face and she looked so sad he wished he dared take her in his arms and give her a reassuring hug. *Just like I'd do for little Sally.*

"How is he today? Does his cough sound any better? Maybe now we're stopped he can get well."

Motioning her out of hearing of the wagon, Lee shook his head. "He sounds worse than last night. I'm going to build a fire to make him some hot coffee and maybe soup."

"Lee, I'm worried about him," Nancy whispered, her blue eyes filled with fear. "He looks so frail. When you get your fire built, I can brew him some licorice root tea. I have other herbs for cough too, Greta showed me ones to pick when we camped by the river."

He gave her a steady smile and although he wanted to squeeze her hand, he clenched his hands in his pockets. Sometimes Nancy welcomed his touch and other times she didn't. He never knew when she wouldn't mind. Best not to rile her. "Then I best get that fire built." He told her about the butter and Nancy brightened a little.

"I'll make them the best biscuits I know how." Even her voice sounded happier. "And we'll make sure Erica and James get some too. Thank you, Lee."

Even though the rain still dripped down in endless misery, the day felt a little sunnier to Lee. He gave Nancy a grin and his heart lurched when she returned one of her own.

Chapter Eighteen

Nancy put on a cheerful face and climbed into the McGregors' wagon; her heart clenched at the raspy sound of Eugene's cough, his gaunt, hollow cheeks. *He sounds so much worse!*

Eugene lay on a pallet of blankets Greta had made by clearing out one corner of the wagon. Although not a big man, he looked so shrunken lying in the nest of covers, Nancy struggled to keep fear from showing on her face. She gritted her teeth and forced a smile on her face. The basket of herbs trembled in her fingers.

"You look all warm and comfortable." Nancy felt like the words mocked them all, but Eugene managed a sickly chuckle. "Snug as a bug in a rug."

A few days before, Greta had made the decision to leave some of their treasures behind. "Eugene needs space to lie down and be comfortable," she'd told Nancy and Josephine. "I want you to help me take things out so I can make him a proper bed."

"Not your pretty rocking chair and clock!" Nancy had protested when Greta dumped them from the back of the wagon to the side of the muddy trail. "You wanted them in your new home. Not the trunk that belonged to your great-grandmother! You cherish them so."

Greta, made of sterner stuff than Nancy thought possible, never gave her belongings a backward glance. "They're just things," she said. "Eugene is more important than that old stuff. There's not room in the wagon for a bed and all that."

Even though Nancy wished she could take Greta's things along, she knew her own wagon was too small to hold any extras. As it was, she tried to be thankful that Uncle, despite his wicked ways, had packed well for traveling to California.

Where would I be if he hadn't? It was a sobering thought.

"I'm sure glad we stopped, aren't you?" Nancy kept her voice bright and pleasant, as much for Greta as for Eugene. In the weeks since she'd joined the wagon train, she'd grown fond of the old couple with their sunny banter and loving care. "Gives us time to sit a spell and get ready for the miles ahead. Just wish it was a mite drier."

Greta sent her a quick, uneasy smile.

"Lee told me about the butter, and I'd be glad to mix up some biscuits. I brought some licorice root along so as soon as Lee gets a fire built, I'll brew you up some tea, Mr. Eugene. It's real handy for coughs."

"It surely is," Greta replied as she tugged the blankets up around Eugene's neck, her voice taking on a false cheery tone too, as if her worst fears were coming true, and she couldn't stop it. "Best thing there is to clear up all that muck in your throat. Now, you just rest, and I'll go out with Nancy to get the butter. You'll be all right, husband?"

Eugene nodded, his weary eyes staring at her. His lips trembled in a slight smile as if he were too weak to do more. The sight crushed Nancy's heart. *What will Greta do if she loses him? It will be like someone ripped out her heart.*

He just has to get better!

Nancy handed her the willow basket and Greta placed it on top of a crate.

"We'll let you rest," Greta motioned Nancy to climb out of the wagon before her.

I sure wish I knew more about doctoring people. Mama had a knack for knowing which herbs or potions to use for what. If Nancy got stung by a bee or burnt her hand on the wood stove, Mama had a sure-enough remedy right at hand. *I wish I'd paid more attention while she was alive to teach me.*

At the Platte, Nancy had walked with Greta and Josephine, picking any herbs they saw that could be useful. They'd found water hyssop and valerian, several others Nancy didn't know. Mama had always been the one to grow and harvest such things. Although she tried to keep her mind on what the older women said, her thoughts had been on other things than herbs.

Like Lee? Finding Mr. Morgan? Although lately here, Mr. Morgan had drifted to the back of her mind more and more.

"Now, let me check that butter," Greta said once they'd left the wagon, "and you can mix up some biscuits. I've got half a kettle of barley soup left over, maybe we can heat that up. All he needs is rest and hot food. He'll soon be fine."

"Best thing is hot food and rest," Nancy agreed, although she noticed how Greta's hand shook as she handed over the pail with the butter.

She's afraid of losing him. Afraid hot soup and rest won't cure him at all.

"You go on now." Greta handed over the sloshy pail of not-quite-churned butter, her fearful eyes glancing back at the wagon. "I'll help you brew the tea when you get that fire built. I—I don't like to leave him too long."

Nancy nodded, heart and throat tight. There were no words she could say.

***

Despite the dull, monotonous gray day, everyone made camp the best they could. They sloshed through mud and picketed the animals. If they had somewhere to graze, the animals didn't seem to mind the drippy sky. Mr. Maxwell had found a camp spot with sparse grass and there was plenty of water coming from the sky.

No loss without some gain, as Mama used to say. We might be drowning, Nancy thought, *but at least we don't have to worry about water.* A small watering hole appeared beside the trail in a natural indentation of the rocks. Rain filled it with fresh, sweet water.

"A gift from the Almighty," Josephine commented when she filled a pail to brew a pot of coffee. "We can fill all our water barrels for the trail ahead."

To Nancy's delight, along about sunset the rain petered out and the most glorious rainbow filled the sky. The brilliant colors stretched from one horizon to the other, lighting up the old brown world with shining beams of hope. She stood in the cool, fresh dusk and watched that colored bow until it faded as evening fell. It lifted her heart somehow—like maybe she could sail into those pale colors all the way to heaven.

After she'd brewed the tea and Greta had made sure Eugene drank enough, the older woman fed him spoonsful of barley soup. Nancy's eyes pooled with tears as the woman fed him so tenderly and hopefully. Although he praised Nancy's biscuits, the old man was clearly too ill to taste more than a few crumbs. Nancy found herself struggling to eat and swallow, her throat taut with unshed tears.

"Let me sit with Eugene for a while," Lee offered after supper. "Now that the rain's done for the night, I've built up a nice campfire. You ladies sit here and relax, dry out."

Greta didn't want to leave her husband, but Lee and Nancy insisted.

"You don't want to get sick too." Nancy's words tipped Greta's reluctance. "Mr. Eugene needs you to keep your strength up for him. You've been nursing him for days. Come sit out by the fire and rest your feet."

Lee put a couple of crates out for them to sit on and when Josephine came by, he brought out one for her too, joking, "the finest in sitting chairs on the California Trail, ladies."

Even Greta managed a small chuckle as they sat before the fire Lee had built from his clothes trunk. A few others had built fires and it was pleasant to sit in the twilight, watching the warm golden flames from the different fires.

Lee's fire smelled sweet and woodsy, a rare contrast to the scent of the buffalo chip fires they were used to having. The wood smoke lifted into the deep blue of the sky, like a big dark bowl overhead with tiny, sparkling chips of stars.

Nancy couldn't stop staring overhead, wondering if Mama might be looking down from heaven. Such a big sky above made her feel small.

"Love is a peculiar thing," Greta almost whispered as they sat near the warmth of the fire. She wore a white shawl and tugged it closer across the bodice of her plaid dress. "I was thinking today how I can't remember my life before I met Eugene and married him. Isn't that strange?"

Josephine, huddled in a gray army blanket, smiled into the orange flames. A twinkle of delight shone in her eyes. "Oh, my yes, not so strange at all. Before I met Ambrose, I was so shy, my mama'd say, 'Josie, if you don't speak up to some boy, you'll never get wed.' But I'd be so scared of any boy who looked my way, my throat would close right up. I figured I'd be an old maid forever until Ambrose looked my way."

Sitting on her crate, warm and snug in a green shawl, Nancy smiled at them both. She had never heard anyone talk about love before. Mama had never shared how she met Papa, or even if she had loved him. Even the few friends Nancy had back in Arkansas hadn't spoken much about love—getting married, having children, yes. But they'd never acted like a person got married for love.

"How did you... how did you know you loved him for sure?" Nancy asked, wishing she could understand this bewildering emotion. "Is it hard to know you're doing the right thing when you get married?"

Josephine chuckled and Greta's smile grew wider. "Now, don't we know who she's thinking about, Greta?"

Suddenly, Nancy wished she hadn't asked the question. *They think I'm asking about Lee.*

"Wonder what it was those two wrote about all the time," Josephine teased, poking at the fire with a slat from Lee's trunk. Sparks flew up and became black embers sailing toward the sky. "That Lee looks like the kind of gent who'd send some right nice letters to a gal he intended to marry."

Hoping Lee couldn't hear the conversation inside McGregor's wagon, Nancy shifted on the crate, uneasy with this unexpected examination.

"Letters?" Oh Lord, now what have I gotten myself into?

Chapter Nineteen

"Didn't you and Lee write love letters, Nancy? Eugene and I must have written enough love notes to burn up a whole forest of trees when we were courting," Greta admitted, her round cheeks glowing in the firelight. A twinkle lit her blue eyes as she folded the edge of her shawl across her stomach. 'Used to save them all, tied with a blue ribbon in my hope chest."

"Ambrose couldn't write." Josephine's face shone with remembrances Nancy couldn't even imagine. "But he showed it in other ways. Didn't Lee write to you, Nancy, telling you where to meet him on the trail? Or did he get word to you some other way? I'd be interested to know."

I don't want to lie. To admit Lee and I didn't write to one another. I wrote to Mr. Morgan, not Lee. Would they think that's wrong? That I answered an ad to be a mail-order bride? Would they think I'm—I'm wanton like Uncle did?

"I ...I ..." Nancy wished she'd never asked the question and thought frantically on how to change the subject. What would Greta and Josie think if she admitted she hadn't known Lee before? *I am wicked!* "Lee... well... I ..."

I don't even know if he can write! Mama had seen to Nancy's schooling when Uncle stopped allowing her to go. But Nancy knew many people didn't know how to read or write. Maybe Lee was one of them.

"Now, let's not tease her." Josie covered the uncomfortable moment as Nancy fidgeted on the hard, wooden crate. "Guess a courting couple's got some privacy coming. If Nancy wants to share what Lee wrote, that's up to her. I'd turn redder than rhubarb when anyone questioned me about Ambrose when we were courting, but I knowed I loved him sure enough."

How? How could you know what love truly is?

Although they'd heard the story before, Greta entertained them a few minutes with the tale of the night she'd met Eugene at a dance. It did Nancy's heart good to see the older woman smile and relax. Nursing her husband had taken some of the starch out of her lately.

"Met my Ambrose when he hired on to work for my pa," Josie remembered. "Mama said she'd met my pa the same way when he hired on to work for *her* pa. A family tradition you might say."

"I wish I'd asked my mama how she met my papa. He died before I was born. Mama never told me how they met."

Oddly, Nancy found herself curious. *Why didn't I ask her things before she died? Did she love Papa? Did the sight of him make her heart do a skip, jump for joy? Just like mine does when I...*

"Didn't she now?" Greta asked, interrupting Nancy's thoughts. "I don't recall you've ever told us much about your life before you joined the train. Is your mama still alive?"

"Oh, no!" Sitting up straighter, Nancy folded her hands in the lap of green calico, relieved to talk about some other subject than Lee Conner. "Mama died when I was twelve."

"Was it sickness?" Josephine questioned.

"No... she..." What did it matter if she told the truth? Uncle was somewhere far, far away and Nancy found herself remembering that difficult time with a catch in her throat. "Mama had taken the spring wagon into town to buy groceries. We lived with my uncle, mama's brother. He was... is... Uncle was a hard man. Everything had to be his way. wanted to go to town with Mama that day, but Uncle said no." Even six years later, Nancy could still remember the last time she'd seen Mama alive. "Mama looked so pretty that morning. She wore the loveliest green dress with a tatted lace collar— she made it herself. Mama did sewing to make money."

Sewed and did alterations until her fingers bled to keep Uncle in money to buy whiskey. Why didn't we leave? Why did we stay?

"Did she look like you, Nancy?"

Nancy laughed at such an outlandish idea. "Oh, no! I'm so plain! She was so pretty—long dark hair, all curly if she didn't put it up in a bun, and the sweetest blue eyes. Mama was prettier than anybody in the world."

Until... Nancy could still remember the shock of seeing Mama's lifeless body in a wooden coffin a few days later. Mama's green dress was gone. When Nancy questioned, the sheriff's wife told Nancy they'd cleaned off all the blood, but Mama had a big hole in her chest. A gun barrel pressed to her bodice had ripped the green dress to shreds and left Mama's blood to pool and stain the wood flooring of the general store.

"Your uncle wouldn't bring another dress decent enough to bury her in," the sheriff's wife had told Nancy in private, anger hardening her face. "Said it would be a waste of good clothes he could sell. I found a dress in the church missionary barrel. I did the best I could, Nancy. I'm sorry."

Nancy remembered thinking it was wrong to bury Mama in such an awful drab dress. Not even her own dress but a borrowed dark blue poplin from a missionary barrel! Not her pretty mama with the sweet voice and the soft hands to wipe away tears or comfort her after one of Uncle's whippings.

It had been a long time since she'd cried about Mama, but Nancy felt warm tears course down her cheeks. A sob caught in her chest and pushed her breath flat, like there was not enough air anywhere to breathe.

"What happened, Nancy?" Greta's voice asked from beyond the fire's glow.

Josephine reached out a gentle hand to place over Nancy's. "Tell us."

"Mama went to town to buy groceries and there was a robbery. A man shot her, even though she didn't do anything. Uncle said… Uncle said it was God's will. But I don't know… why God would want my mama to die."

It was a question she'd pondered for years. *Mama was just in the wrong place at the wrong time. I should have been with her. But Uncle had to have his way! Why wasn't Uncle the one who died? He killed mama forcing her to go that day!*

"Now, I don't believe that at all," Greta spoke with more spunk than she had since Eugene had gotten ill. "I think a lot of folks say that to explain things that happen. But I've seen a lot in my life and I think there's bad things that happen because there's bad folks in this world. It might make them feel better to think God's somewhere dealing out all the hurt and sorrow—but I figure God's got better things to do than worry about every little thing that happens to the likes of us."

"You're right," Josephine agreed, the firelight soft on her face. "I never figured it was God's will my Ambrose got shot. It was two greedy claim jumpers who wanted what he'd worked for. If God had a hand in anything it was having my Matthew be off that day, so he didn't get killed too. Way, I looked at it, God was somewheres cryin' His heart out too when my Ambrose got killed."

I never thought of it that way.

142

"I... always believed what Uncle said," Nancy almost whispered, pondering this strange turn of thought in her mind. Mama had never said it was "God's will" for her papa to die. It had just been something that happened in life. People lived and people died. Some were sweet like Mama and others were as mean and hateful as Uncle. *Could that be true?*

"Not all men tell the truth, Nancy," Greta said in a soft, caring voice. "Maybe your uncle truly believed that, but it didn't make it so. You're young yet, but one day you'll understand that you have to make up your own mind about some things in life."

Could Greta be right? If Uncle didn't speak the truth about God, was he wrong about the things he'd called her too?

I never thought it was wrong to write to Mr. Morgan. Not after Susie Cummings told me about men who advertised for marriageable women. Susie didn't think it was wrong.

"They're called mail-order brides and there's whole catalogs of men who put in ads. One of my aunts on Papa's side, she wrote to a man in Oregon. He sent her passage to come out and they got married! She said it was a mite strange at first, being married to a man she didn't know all that well. But, they had four children and now they have a big lumber business. Aunt Maeve says she's happier than she's ever been."

But Uncle said it was wrong when he found the letters. He screamed and hollered and cursed at how wicked I was. Mama always said Uncle knew best, but did he?

For the first time, Nancy questioned the past as the other women stopped talking and sat in quiet contentment around the campfire.

Maybe it's all right to travel on and find Mr. Morgan. Although...

Nancy's heart gave a lurch when she thought about Lee. Surely having thoughts for two men at once was wicked. Only a wanton woman would care for two men at once.

Chapter Twenty

"We're going to have to move forward." Trevor stood beside Lee's water-logged wagon as the rain sluiced down. Thinner than when they'd left Independence a few months earlier, Trevor now wore perpetual worry lines across his tanned forehead. His calm voice had grown sharper, more harried the more miles they traveled. He had admitted to Lee and no one else that this journey had been harder than any other. "There's just no other way. No telling how long these storms will last and we're losing time. If we don't get over the Rockies before winter . . ."

No one wanted to think of the sobering possibility. Everyone had heard of the Donner Party and their tragic ending. The same fate could await them if they were trapped in the snow.

The men of the train had gotten together the evening before. With no hope of building a fire in the constant downpour, they shared a diminishing store of dried fruit and drank watery milk from the McGregor's cows, as they discussed options. The main solution was the one Trevor shared again this morning.

Move along or die.

"It's going to be hard going," Lee answered his friend, wishing he still had the makings of a cigarette to offer him or even one of Danny's licorice sticks. Anything to bring back a spark to Trevor's eyes. He looked like he had the world on his shoulders.

Reckon he has for sure—our world anyway.

"If only this blasted rain would let up..." Trevor sighed, a deep sigh pulled from way down in his chest.

Another day, another deluge. Lee had forgotten what it felt like to be dry. Dampness invaded the wagons; even the flour in the barrels had gotten wet as water seeped through cracks in the wooden barrels. It smelled musty just like the cornmeal and sugar. Beans swelled and mildew had to be scraped off the rinds of slab bacon. Still, it was food, and they'd need to eat it no matter what. Eat moldy food or starve. Even Danny, young as he was, knew better than to complain.

"I sure will be glad to get to Fort Laramie, won't you, Lee?" he'd asked the night before as they hunkered in the narrow confines of the wagon, the dreary patter of raindrops hitting the canvas. "Mr. Smith says they got a store there where we can buy just about anything we want."

"That so?" Lee had asked just to be sociable, knowing store-bought goods would take more of his diminishing coins. He'd have to restock some foodstuffs. He'd left Independence with 150 pounds of flour and 25 pounds of salt. Both barrels were dangerously low and damp.

Having to feed Danny and Nick and share with the Richards—although they were a little touchy about accepting—had brought him almost to the bottom of the barrels. Coffee was long gone, as well as half his dried beans. The rest were soggy and bloated after a night when the canvas split and dumped a waterfall into the muslin bag.

This morning, talking with Trevor, Lee shivered in wet trousers as he looked around at the sorry lot of wagons. *Last week we were complaining about the heat. Sure wish we had some of that warmth today. Sweat or drown.*

Everyone had huddled in cramped wagons or under tents for the past three days. Each time they thought the storms had stopped; another came along. The road was mired in mud and just looking at it Lee's heart quailed.

"I'm going to have everyone go through their wagons and lighten the loads. The less the animals have to pull through this quagmire, the easier it will be." Trevor said in a firm voice, although Lee could sense the distress behind the words. "People are getting short on supplies. Once that happens, it's harder to keep people's spirits up. Sure wish we could get some fresh game. I guess even the animals are hunkered down until the rain lets up."

Mr. Maxwell had gone out scouting the day before. He'd galloped back to announce there were some antelopes not far off. Lee had gone hurting with the other men, eager for fresh game to supplement their dwindling supplies. Sadly, they'd come back empty handed, wetter if possible, and more discouraged.

"What about the McGregors?" Lee asked. "When I went by this morning, Eugene was awful weak. He can't drive his wagon. Do you think Freddy might?"

"No. I asked him earlier. He's going to ride the Morgan and travel with Hanna. Once we get to the fort, he plans to sell his oxen or trade them to old man Kelsey. He said he's not sure Eugene doesn't have cholera and he wants to stay away just in case."

Lee snorted. "Cholera! He's not that sick. It's just a cough or croup from so much damp. He's just weak, is all, he needs time to rest."

"Lee, you know as well as I do that time is something we don't have a lot of out here. We're all low on food. I heard some grumbles about killing one of the McGregor's cows. People are running low on supplies, and we need to get to the fort to stock up. Once we get there, we're only a third of the way to California."

Only a third!

"Is there anyone else who can drive Eugene's wagon?"

"No, it's going to take everyone to keep pulling these wagons out of the mud. I think the only thing we could do is try to get Greta and Eugene to ride in someone else's wagon, leave theirs behind."

"Can't we wait—just until Eugene can drive his own wagon?" Lee asked. "I know Greta's not strong enough but surely, once he rests…"

Trevor frowned and shook his head. "We have to move on. I'm sorry, Lee, that's how it has to be."

Lee knew the McGregors wouldn't want to leave everything they owned behind. Greta had already tossed out some of her treasures to lighten the load. They still had some barrels of food, tools to begin their lives in California, a dozen other things it would be hard to shift to someone else's wagon. *We're all crammed as it is.* "There has to be another way."

"Well," Trevor looked off in the distance. "I don't like saying this—but I guess if you want to stay on until Eugene can travel, you can. We can't wait up for you, but we'll stay over at the fort a day or so, and you might catch up."

Alone out here! Lee's heart dropped. Thomas would do it in a heartbeat, but he knew he wasn't as brave as his friend. Still, what other choice did he have? No one else would offer.

"Let me talk to them and see what they say," Lee compromised.

He tugged a sodden collar around his equally wet neck and headed toward the McGregor wagon. The mud sucked his boots in deep with each step and his legs ached just going the short distance. *How can we drive in this?* Buttercup mooed a greeting from her picket rope, and he stopped to give the cow a pat to her skinny side. The trail had been hard on the cow; there had been only scanty milk for a few days now.

Eugene's cough rattled in his chest. To Lee, it sounded ominous. He'd heard some of the orphans cough like this... right before they died. In his heart, he knew Eugene could not possibly get better. Maybe Greta knew too.

Greta looked up at him, her face thinner and paler than it had been when they first started out. Worry for Eugene had eaten away at her jovial good humor and dulled her blue eyes into pools of misery. For the past three days, she'd sat beside Eugene's pallet, holding her husband's frail hand in hers. Cajoling, talking, willing him to live.

"Trevor thinks it best we move on."

"Ach, in this rain?" Greta asked. "And how are we to drive our poor oxen through such mud? Is Mr. Scott going to drive our wagon again? I don't like to say anything—it was generous of him to offer—but he's not a bit careful to avoid all the jolts and jars. Eugene needs quiet to get well."

Lee's smile felt false even to himself. "Well, now, you won't have to worry about that. Freddy's going on with Hanna, he won't be driving your wagon."

"Then how are we to move on?"

"Trevor had a thought," Lee said, although he knew what the answer would be. "Maybe we could put you and Eugene into one of the other wagons, divvy up your supplies so we could all go on. Once we reach the fort maybe we can..."

Greta's eyes narrowed in thought but her answer came quick enough. "No. We can't let others put out for us. And what are we to do in California with nothing to start a new life? We have no savings. We sold the farm to begin again. We've seed and tools, the cows. Is there no other way?"

149

Only if I stay here. And what am I supposed to do with Danny and Nancy and... Nick? How did I get saddled with all this responsibility?

"Trevor suggested I could wait behind with you. They'll be at the fort a few days; we have a good chance to catch up. Once Eugene is better..."

If that happens.

"I can drive your wagon into the fort."

"But you've responsibilities of your own, Lee." Greta kneaded her husband's bony hand, distress in her voice. "We can't let you do such a thing. There must be another way."

There is no other way! Frustrated, Lee wanted to shout, to curse even though he'd never cursed in his life. Mr. Montgomery had come down hard on that vice. Thomas had felt the sting of his switch often enough for curse words. Suddenly, from thousands of miles away, Lee thought with longing of the Mississippi Orphanage and Mr. Montgomery's wisdom. No matter the changes Lee had seen, Mr. Montgomery knew how to take care of people with nothing more than prayer and a bootlace. *What would you do? I sure wish I could talk to you and ask.*

"Let me go talk to the others," Lee eased himself out of the wagon, smelling of sickness and death.

***

"No, I say!" Freddy Scott shouted, glaring around at the circle of men, "I say leave them here! They knew the risks when they came along. Eugene is at death's door now. Why should we endanger our lives to stay behind?"

"It would be the Christian thing to do," Josie murmured from the crowd. She and Nancy stood side by side with a couple of the other women. Although Lee knew them all by name after so many months on the trail, he didn't often talk to many of them. Mrs. Appleton, who had given him a small jar of raspberry jam she'd made when Danny played with her colicky baby one afternoon. Mr. Kelsey's sour-faced wife who said as little as possible to anyone. Hanna, wearing a rain poncho and studying the crowd with an unreadable expression on her face.

"That's so," little Mrs. Appleton agreed, although a sharp glance from her tall, bony husband stopped her from speaking more.

"Freddy's right," Mr. Appleton snapped. "Everyone knew the risks when they came on the trail. The McGregors made their bed, let them lie in it. We've got children to feed and I'm running low on food. I say we move on."

"Me too!"

"Yup!"

To no one's surprise, Spence and Virgil stepped to stand by Freddy's side, nodding in agreement. To Lee's absolute shock, Trevor nodded his head too. "He's right, Lee, we all knew the risks when we came out here. Ted Maxwell and I were discussing this and we decided we must keep moving. There is no other way."

If Lee had been asked to speak to save his life just then, he wouldn't have managed. Having Trevor take Freddy's side felt like the worst betrayal in the world. *I trusted him. I thought he was my friend.* Every so often around the campfires at night, Trevor had spoken to Lee about possibly joining him on another wagon train. He'd hinted he could always use a good man to help hunt or scout or just tend to the wagons. It had been an idea Lee pondered if things didn't work out in

California. Now, he felt betrayed, as if Trevor had been just spouting words.

Trevor's next words soothed over the hurt, although to Lee they opened another problem. "I've been thinking, though. You're going to be hard-pressed to drive two wagons once Eugene's on the mend, and Danny's too young to drive yours. I thought maybe Nick can drive your wagon. That way, you'll meet us at the fort when you catch up."

Nick? A blind man drive my wagon?

Chapter Twenty-One

Lee had never been at such a loss for words before. His throat closed tight, and he knew he'd never be able to come up with a good explanation to give those harsh, unfeeling faces glaring at him and Trevor for the suggestion.

Lee saw the ugly truth in their faces. They didn't want to have this conversation, to make this decision. They wanted to press on and leave it behind, faces forward. The same way they passed the bleached carcasses alongside the trail and the unknown graves; faces forward not to acknowledge the harsh reality.

Several times during the storms, when Danny had been visiting the Richards, Lee had tried to speak to Nick about his infirmity. There had been snatched bits of conversation, but Lee always felt Nick had to be hiding some truth.

"I'm blind. What else is there to say?"

"There's plenty," Lee had whispered, frustrated by Nick's lack of response to his hurried questions. "How did you find us on the trail? Did someone lead you to us?" *Are you a bandit? A robber?* "A blind person can't see. I saw how you tried to grab that rope the night of the storm. How could you ride a horse and do the things you do without sight?"

How did you know someone killed your family? How did you bury them?

"I'm able to discern some shapes, light and dark." Nick explained. "Pegasus is a very intelligent horse. He's never let me leave a path yet or fall into danger."

"What about it, Lee? If Nick takes your wagon on ahead?"

ZACHARY MCCRAE

"Danny can ride with me," Nancy chimed in, pressing to the front of the crowd, her blue eyes searching his for approval.

Yes, that's what my betrothed would do, offer to take my little brother to safety. Except she's not really my betrothed—and I've never gotten to talk to her alone either. How do I know Danny will be safe with her? But, what am I thinking—Nick can't drive a wagon!

Lee looked at all the faces surrounding him—only a few of them sympathetic like James Richards' and Nancy's.

Before he could figure out how to break the news, Danny pushed to the front of the crowd to stand beside Lee. Rivulets of water ran down his hollow cheeks and he blurted out, "Nick can't drive our wagon. He can't see." Just like he was quoting common knowledge, Danny said, "He's blind."

"Blind?" Freddy's eyes widened in incredulity; his ugly mouth pressed into an enraged look of scorn. Raindrops dripped down his quivering cheeks. "How did you manage to saddle us with someone else that's a burden? A blind man, McGregor—who knows if he's going to spread cholera to the lot of us? You brought those..." he glanced at James Richards and uttered a slur that caused several of the women to gasp. James's face grew tight, and Lee noticed how he clenched his hands to his side. "Now you've brought another liability on us! I say we all move out and leave you and your friends here." The word "friends" was spoken in a hateful sneer.

"Lee?" Trevor eyed him as if he couldn't fathom the situation. The betrayed expression on the older man's face cut Lee to the quick. *Trevor depends on me. He's even asked me if I'd consider joining on one day as a trail boss.* "I don't understand. Why didn't you speak up earlier?"

Danny had no qualms about explaining; the child knew no better and thought everyone was as curious as he was. "Lee said he had a problem, so I asked him, and Mr. Nick said he's blind. He can see shapes and sometimes light and dark," Danny explained to the faces who stared with various expressions of fear, belligerence, or intolerance. "I don't think he can drive our wagon though. Do you, Lee?"

Lee shook his head, unsure how to explain or even if he wanted to.

"Lee?" Trevor questioned, hurt.

"I didn't know at first," Lee fumbled for an explanation. "And after that, what was I supposed to do? Leave a blind man alone out here? This country is harsh enough for those of us who can see."

"I say we leave them all out here!" Spence shouted. "Let's move on while we can!"

Freddy joined in and several more people agreed with him, including the Appleton's and Kelsey's. Hanna stood halfway between Freddy's crowd and the few sympathetic people standing near Lee. Angry murmurs passed through the crowd.

"I've had enough!" Freddy shouted, working up the crowd to a fever pitch, "Trevor and Lee destroyed my wagon–"

"That's not true!" Surprisingly, the shout came from Nancy, those blue eyes blazing as she stepped forward, hands on the hips of her green calico, stepping to Lee's side as if she planned to defend his honor. "You were smoking and dropped a cigar. You started the fire. You can't blame Lee or Trevor for that."

"They could have saved more of my merchandise, but they didn't!" Freddy ignored the blame and glared at Nancy, "I'm through with this wagon train. Let the rest of you stay here while the old man dies and get along with a kid and a blind man if you want, who wants to join me?"

Many of the people stepped forward and agreed with Freddy. Trevor stood off to the side, undecided at this development. Lee could see the expression on his face—Trevor was torn at the conflict and worried about the people he'd taken under his care in Independence. Ted Maxwell was somewhere on the trail ahead, scouting their route past Chimney Rock and Scott's Bluff. The decision to stay or leave would rest on Trevor's shoulders, and Lee could see the way it weighed on him. *More and more I know how he feels.*

"Go!" Nancy shouted, "I'm standing with Lee. He's been good to all of us. He's helped me every second since you all allowed me to join your train. He's helped all of you." She glared around at the faces of the people. "You, Hanna, he helped you when Freddy tossed you out of his wagon."

Lee gulped, unaware that she'd known that.

"He treated you decent and not many on this train did!"

Hanna had the grace to look ashamed and stepped further away from Freddy.

"And you," she pointed to several others, listing small chores he'd done for each of them. Lee flushed. Had Nancy really been watching him that close? "Lee's done nothing but help and this is the thanks he gets. You all want to turn on him because he took in someone else? Well, frankly, I wouldn't want to travel with people who'd toss a blind man out in this desolate country. You're as bad as the Donners. I'm staying with Lee! If we have to abandon one of our wagons to help the McGregors we will. The rest of you ought to be ashamed."

A few of Freddy's crowd murmured and complained but gave Nancy mutinous glances. Several other people looked ashamed.

Josephine stepped forward. "I wouldn't have Mark if Lee hadn't saved him from the river. We'll travel with Lee and be glad he's such a good man. He might be young, but he's kind and generous and I know he wouldn't abandon me on the trail."

"Me too!" Danny shouted, "I'm sticking with my brother." Little Mark chimed in, "Me too."

To everyone's surprise, Hanna stepped away from Freddy. "I guess I'm staying here too and traveling with Lee, Freddy."

"You're a fool," he snarled and gave her a push that caused her to stumble. Josephine reached out to steady her and gave Hanna an uncertain smile.

James Richards glared but then spoke in his quiet, steady voice, "Wasn't ever any question me and Erica will join you, Lee. No matter who else does."

The men broke off and began to discuss what to do.

"I say let's travel on with Freddy," Mr. Kelsey said, his eyes full of accusation. "We're losing time every second we let someone else slow us down." There were shouts, angry recriminations, and accusations. Trevor tried to soothe over the frayed emotions, stepping in to state how they'd all signed on to travel with him. Watching the struggle, Lee understood exactly how he felt. He'd felt it many times when the other orphans clustered around him, each with a different idea of how things should be done.

"Everyone, listen, we need to talk about this calmly and reasonably," Trevor shouted to be heard over the growing volume of voices, "none of you know this land like Ted

Maxwell or I do. You don't want to go off halfcocked and end up following the wrong path. Let's all try to figure out how to do this together."

"No!" Freddy shouted, "We're moving on!" He gave Lee a look full of vengeance, although Lee couldn't figure out how any of this was his fault. *I'd stay behind even if Freddy was ill. Or, I'd hope I had enough decency to do that.*

In the end, Freddy, Spence, Virgil and three other wagons left the train. They lumbered slowly through the deep mud. The ones left behind watched them for almost three hours as they labored across the rocks and mud. It was slow going but maybe the others felt some relief to move on. They were inches closer to California.

To Lee's gratitude, Trevor decided to stay behind.

I wouldn't have any idea which way to travel if he hadn't.

"Nancy's right, Lee," Trevor said, "I don't know what Mr Maxwell will decide, but I'm going to stick with those of you in this train. If we don't get through the Rockies, we'll build a cabin and figure out a way to survive until spring. We'll stick together. I'd like to think if I was down and out like Nick or Nancy, you'd stop on the trail for me too. That's what makes a man—a person who's willing to put their life on the line for others. You think of others first, Lee."

Lee gulped, but Trevor's words helped him to feel stronger. *Thomas, I feel like maybe I'm becoming the man you always told me I could be.* For just a second, he was reminded of Mr Montgomery too, the way he'd always said, "one day, you'll be a man we can all be proud of, Lee."

Toward evening, Eugene's cough grew worse. The rain stopped just as sunset washed across the western sky, a brilliant orange, yellow, pink swatch of colors and hope. Lee broke up another crate that had held grain to build a fire. He tried not to be dismayed at the emptiness of his supplies. *How will I feed Danny if we run out of food?*

"I'll make some tea from these herbs," Nancy said as she used rainwater she'd collected in a tin pail. "Maybe Eugene can drink some."

"We can hope," Josie said as she stirred a pot of stew. Earlier, Mr. Maxwell had ridden in with two plump jackrabbits to share with those left behind. If he was upset at Freddy's group going ahead, he didn't say much. Just accepted a cup of very weak chicory coffee and went off to talk privately with Trevor.

Eugene's cough rattled worse throughout the evening. About midnight, as the stars twinkled in a deep blue velvet sky, he took a final breath and died.

"No! No! No!" Greta's shriek woke everyone who'd managed to get a fitful sleep. Lee and Nancy had sat with her in the cramped wagon. Nancy holding Greta's hand, Lee keeping the death watch and stirring each time Eugene coughed.

Greta was inconsolable.

The next morning, Lee, James, and Trevor managed to dig a grave in the muddy ground. They wrapped Eugene in a Hudson Bay blanket and lowered him into the earth beside the trail. Greta wept and screamed while Josie and Nancy tried their best to calm her. When they'd patted the mound of earth over Eugene, everyone, even the children, walked around to find rocks to pile over the grave.

"It may keep the animals away for a while," Trevor whispered to Lee, "but most of the time they find the bodies. Just a fact of life out here."

Lee shuddered inside, trying to keep from imagining Eugene being pulled from his final resting place by coyotes or wolves. Nancy insisted they write Eugene's name on a piece of rawhide and place it through a stick to mark the place. "Maybe someday Greta can come back and bury him proper."

No one believed her. When they'd buried Eugene, Trevor mounted his black stallion and shouted out, "Wagons, HO!" Hanna had offered to drive Greta's wagon, since she had none of her own. Despite Greta's talk about Hanna not being respectable, she didn't seem to mind. Her blue eyes, dull and missing a spark, stared ahead at the trail as if she'd rather be beside Eugene in his grave.

They were back on the trail, mired in mud every few feet and making slow progress. But the sun was shining, and they were headed in the direction of Fort Laramie. *I hope I can figure out how to buy some more supplies. I wonder if we'll run into Freddy when we get there.*

Lee had an eerie feeling that they hadn't seen the last of Freddy Scott. Not if the vengeful look he'd narrowed at Lee as he left was any indication.

Chapter Twenty- Two

"Help!"

A woman's scream jolted Lee from a fitful slumber. A gun shattered the night with a series of powerful retorts, and the scent of gun smoke wafted on the cooling night breezes. Horses whinnied and stamped, jerking at the picket ropes.

"Get away! You leave me alone!"

Another shot that must have hit home. A thud and a deep groan. A man's voice, "Get the horses! Now! I'm hit!"

"Lee!" Danny whimpered in fear. "What's happening?"

Lee stumbled out from under the wagon, hearing Nick thrashing around inside and trying to get out. "What's wrong?" he called out. "Who is shooting?"

"Stay here! I'm going to find out."

It was so dark Lee could only see shapes and shadows. Again, a woman screamed, and he realized it was Nancy's voice! Without yanking on his boots, he grabbed the Henry and ran to the front of his wagon. They'd made camp the night before and Nancy's wagon was several past his. The wagon before him held Hanna and Greta. Hanna, clutching a threadbare, dusty robe, leaned out of Greta's wagon. "What's wrong? Who's screaming?"

"Nancy," Lee said in a terse voice, stumbling as he stubbed his toe on a rock. Pain shot up his leg, but he kept running.

Again, gunfire shattered the air and someone—this time a man—hollered. "Go!"

Before Lee could quite figure out what was happening a wagon and team passed him, moving at a fast clip. No wonder! A man sitting on the wagon seat raised the whip to hurry a team of horses along. It snapped over the backs of two horses Lee recognized as they galloped past, almost knocking him down. Beauty and Cletus!

"Hey!" He started after the wagon, raised the Henry, and then lowered it as the wagon clattered over the trail ruts and took off in the night. Somewhere down the trail, the bucket of axle grease tied to the side snapped loose and splattered on the rocky path. A few pings echoed as pots and pans left sitting on the wagon bed bounced out and clattered to a stop.

By now others were gathering around in their night clothes, questions ringing in the air as he found Nancy, holding a smoking Colt, a look of utter disgust on her face. The white nightgown she wore had been torn along the sleeve and there were marks on her face as if someone had slapped her. "Nancy, are you all, right? What happened?" It was clear Nancy's wagon had been taken—there was a bare spot on the trodden down grass, the picket rope cut and just the remains of a campfire to indicate she'd camped for the night.

Josie pressed up close, tugging a flannel nightgown and robe close to her chest. "Nancy, girl! What was all that about? Why would anyone take your wagon?"

"I heard shooting, who was it?" Trevor asked, hurrying up with his gun. "I'm sorry, I was on guard duty, but I guess I nodded off."

Lee hurried to Nancy. Not caring if she got angry, he put his arms around her and pulled her close, just as if she were Sally's age and needed comforting. "Tell me. Who took your wagon?"

Her breath came in short, ragged spurts but she managed to mumble out, "F-freddy and his men. They tried..." She looked at the ripped gown, bare shoulder peeking through, and pushed back her tumble of dark hair. "Freddy tried to assault me—but he didn't realize I always sleep with my Colt."

"That was you shooting?" Josie asked.

Nancy grinned, despite her disheveled appearance. "If there's one thing my uncle taught me worthwhile, it was how to shoot. I'm a fair shot too, did most of the hunting for game because Uncle was too lazy. I guess that Spence never expected me to shoot while he was hitching up my wagon. I—I—Freddy climbed into my wagon and he..." As if noticing Danny and Mark pressed close to Josie, she shook her head and stopped what she'd been about to say. "He tried to kiss me, but I fought him off. Slapped him right hard too. I got the Colt out and he sure backed out of the wagon in a hurry."

Nancy looked back at where her wagon had been. Her face fell and she stammered, "My wagon... they took my wagon and everything. Beauty... Mama gave her to me."

"Why did they take your wagon?" Trevor asked, sounding outraged that he hadn't been able to prevent this latest mishap.

When Nancy shuddered, Lee gave her a reassuring one-sided hug. "Freddy said... he said... let me see how it was to do without, just like him. He said, let Lee take care of me. If wouldn't go with w-with him."

Josie moved forward to pull Nancy into her arms, pushing Lee aside. The whole episode hit Nancy and she leaned into Josie's capable arms and sobbed, "Everything's gone. All my food and supplies. My money. What will I do?"

"Shush, shush, it will look better in the morning."

"How? How?" Nancy's voice grew shrill as she held tight to the older woman's waist.

"Now, you just come along with me," Josie murmured, "it will all look better in the morning."

Lee didn't know why he offered. As he spoke the words, his face flamed, and he realized maybe he sounded too forward. *What would Mr. Montgomery say?* "No, I think it's best she stays with me tonight. In case Freddy comes back." He held up the Henry. "Trevor can get some rest and I'll stand guard."

"I reckon she should be with someone who can protect her," Josie said, although her dark eyes gave him a doubtful glance. "You are betrothed and all..."

I've got to take more time to question her about how she got left on the trail. We've traveled all these miles and all I really know about Nancy is that she was born in Arkansas and her pa died before she was born.

"Danny, you come in with me and Mark then," Josie decided. "I reckon you all got Nick to chaperone. Would that be all right, Trevor?"

Trevor winked. "I'm sure it would. We've had enough excitement for tonight. Nancy, we'll try to see if we can find your wagon tomorrow—or your horse. I'm not sure why Freddy would want to steal from you—you don't have any more than anyone else. Although maybe he figures he can buy more stock when he gets to Fort Laramie. James, if you take guard duty for a few hours, I'll take over for you at two. And I'll have Mr. Morison stand guard at the other end of the wagons. You just protect Nancy, Lee."

"Sounds like Freddy took her wagon to be mean," Josie muttered as she herded Danny and Mark back to her wagon.

They went back to the wagon, Lee uncomfortably aware that Nancy would have to bed down under the wagon on Danny's pallet. "I'm sorry there's not room in the wagon – I could try to shift some things around if you want to sleep in

165

there. But Nick's been sleeping inside. I figured it's easier for him to have less space to roam at night."

Nancy shook her head. "I'm so tired I don't care where I lie down. I think I'd feel better being outside a wagon. When Freddy came into my wagon and tried..." she shuddered and blinked back tears. "I'd just as soon not feel trapped."

Lee showed her Danny's pallet, worried about how close it was to his. *Well, she will probably be asleep when I lie down later.*

"Lee, what's happened?" Nick asked as he climbed out of the back of the wagon.

Giving Nancy some privacy to get settled down under the wagon, Lee built up a campfire to sit watch awhile. In whispers, he explained the situation to Nick. As he settled on a crate almost empty of cornmeal, Nick pulled up a wooden box and sat beside the warm flames. "I'll keep you company if I may."

As the wood caught and sent out warmth, stray embers floated upward, the crackling loud and crisp in the night. Lee held the rifle across his knees and stared into the flames. The fire must have put Nick in a talkative mood.

"Many years ago, before I met my Annabelle, I used to court a lovely lass named Truly. She had bright yellow hair and the most beguiling green eyes. I'm so thankful that I didn't lose my sight until later in life."

"How exactly did you lose your sight, Nick?"

"Oh, that's a story for another night, too long to tell." Nick sighed. "Truly was my first love. First love is a wondrous thing, Lee, don't ever underestimate its power. I may not be able to see, but I can tell you and Nancy belong together."

"Me and Nancy? Oh, no—you don't understand..." Lee shifted on the crate as his hands clenched the rifle. "Nancy and me..."

"You never met until you found her on the trail. She told me."

She did! "What else did she tell you?" He kept his voice low, conscious of Nancy sleeping just a few feet away.

"A great many things about her life, things she will share with you soon. You must remember to listen with your heart, Lee, and not just with your ears. Even though I can't see with my eyes, there are other ways to see things. Trust me in this—you and Nancy belong to one another. She thinks her heart belongs to another, but she will learn. So will you. First love is powerful and sometimes right. Perhaps, if I had followed my heart, I'd have stayed with Truly. There are times when God shows us a clear path to follow, but because we are so certain we know best, we ignore His signs."

Confused, Lee stared through the flames at Nick. Firelight flickered across his face, light and shadows, his sightless eyes almost closed. *Why would he tell me such things? All I feel about Nancy right now is confused. I sure don't think we are destined to truly become betrothed.*

"Do you believe in God, Lee?"

Lee thought of the orphanage, going to Sunday School every week, Mr. Montgomery reading the Good Book at night. "I—I guess so. I guess everyone does, don't they?"

Nick shook his head sadly. "No, not everyone. I think people forget that there's someone holding us all in the palm of His hand. We forget to trust in things we can't see." A smile flickered across his face. "Me, I don't have that option."

"I 'spect you're right." *What an unusual man.* Yet, there was something about him – comforting somehow and reassuring. Like talking to Old Sam. *Maybe now's the time to ask him about getting robbed on the trail and what happened. He's still never explained all that yet.* Just as he opened his mouth to ask, Nick began to speak again.

"Thank you for everything you've done for me, Lee. Not many would pick up a blind man from the trail and care for him as you did. Bless you, young man. You must always remember that with mutual trust people can accomplish a great deal together. Mr. Scott forgot that or perhaps never learned to trust others. You and the others trust Trevor to lead you to California. That is good. He's a trustworthy man, as you are."

"Me? I'm just trying to do what's right. Take care of the folks who trust me." Lee shifted, uncomfortable. Tonight, he felt far from trustworthy. *I couldn't protect Nancy. Or keep Trevor from losing half his wagon train. I'm not even certain I'll be able to keep Danny and me from starving before we get to California.*

"*Exactly. Rather like those men in the Scriptures who were tested by visitors who turned out to be... more. They tried to do what was right, too.*" Nick took a slow breath and situated himself more comfortably on his box. "Now, you go on and go to sleep. You will need your rest tomorrow as we reach Fort Laramie. Perhaps we will even find Freddy Scott."

Lee hesitated. He couldn't deny feeling so weary his eyelids kept sliding shut. "I guess I could. James and Mr. Morison are sitting watch, but I thought maybe if there were more of us. . ."

"There is no need for you to stay awake. My hearing is quite acute. Go rest. I will listen and wake you if I hear anything strange. Tomorrow, perhaps it will be time for me to move on."

Lee figured they'd already had all the excitement they'd have for the night. *Trevor will be awake in a little while anyway.* "Where would you go, Nick? You don't have to leave on account of what anyone says." Lee yawned. "We can talk about it in the morning."

Lee crawled into his pallet, aware of Nancy just a few inches away. He was too sleepy to care. He yawned and drifted into sleep, at some point in the night, he woke to find Nancy had rolled close to him and put her arm across his middle. It gave him an odd feeling. *This isn't right – we aren't married.* But Lee couldn't deny he wished they were, that Nancy was sharing his bed in their home and not huddled under a wagon. *Could Nick be right? Could Nancy be my wife one day?* It was a startling thought but not an unwelcome one. Having Nancy touch him stirred feelings he'd never thought he'd have.

A few minutes later, Nancy woke up startled, pulled her arm away, and turned away from him. Lee held his breath in the dark, not letting her know he'd enjoyed that delicate arm cradling him.

In the morning, just as mysteriously as they'd arrived, Nick and Pegasus were gone.

Chapter Twenty-Three

"Maybe he rode on ahead to the fort," Nancy said as she fried the last of his bacon on the campfire, careful to avoid looking at him too closely. All her clothes had vanished in the wagon, so she'd borrowed a dress from Josie. The bright red calico had faded from too many washings to a light pink. It was so big on Nancy; she'd had to cut off most of the hem and the sleeves kept rolling down to cover her hands "Although I don't know why he wouldn't just wait for us. I still can't see how a blind man could ride along a trail alone."

"No, I don't think so. He said it might be time for him to travel on, but it doesn't sit right with me. Why leave now?" Lee shook his head, remembering Nick's strange conversation from the night before. "There was something—unusual about him. Nancy, do you believe in angels? Or God?"

"I'm not certain. Mama did—but I ain't seen no evidence." Nancy flipped slices of bacon onto a tin plate. Moving the iron spider over the flames, she placed the tin coffee pot of water on to boil. There was no coffee left, but they'd found wild chicory and made do. It was bitter, but better than nothing. "What are you thinking? Why would God show up on our wagon train dressed like Nick?"

Lee shook his head. "I'm not certain. Maybe he didn't."

Just thinking of Nick left him with an odd feeling he couldn't explain. "There's so much I don't understand. Why did he come? Why did he leave?"

Trevor walked up, holding a tin mug of chicory coffee, "Lee, Nancy, I'm going to hold a meeting in a few minutes, gather everyone around. Can you join us? We have to talk about last night." He moved on down the wagon train, stopping at each wagon with the news.

Lee stared at Nancy, who shoved back her tumble of brown curls and gave him a curious look from those cornflower blue eyes. "I'm sorry," she whispered, "this is all my fault."

"How?"

Nancy just shook her head as if she had the weight of the world on her shoulders. He thought, but couldn't be certain, she whispered, "Because I'm so wicked."

***

"I'm afraid our lives are in danger," Mr. Morison was the first to speak up when they'd all assembled near the center of the wagons. "We should never have stood against Freddy Scott to begin with. What's to keep him from coming in the night and taking any of our wagons? Or killing us all in our sleep?"

The crowd murmured, fear traveling as fast as wildfire among some of the women and more than a few of the men.

"I don't think that's so," Trevor said as he looked to Lee for support. More and more the older man had seemed to trust Lee's judgment, something Lee found hard to understand. *I don't know any more than anyone else.* Yet, it made him feel good to know Trevor depended on him just like Mr. Montgomery always had. "Freddy was angry at me and Lee, not any of the rest of you."

"Then why did he take Nancy's wagon?" Mrs. Templeton asked. A gray-haired widow traveling with her older son, Frankie, she'd mostly stayed by herself on the trail.

Lee stepped up, "He wanted Nancy, that's why. And he wanted to get back at me and Trevor for not saving his merchandise. He doesn't have any quarrel with the rest of you."

"You sound pretty certain, young man," Mr. Morison said not unkindly, his bushy eyebrows narrowed, "but you're young yet. You don't know how evil people can be. I'm not sure Freddy wasn't right. You saddled us with a lot of people who can only drag us behind out here. And now this Nick fellow is gone. Where'd he go? Maybe he wasn't blind. Maybe he was here scouting us out and now he's gone back to his gang. We might all be dead before we take our next breath if they're lying in wait. Why should we trust anything you say?"

"I trust him." Trevor said in his firm, commanding voice. "Lee may be young, but he's wiser than some of us. He cares for others too."

Suddenly, Lee felt courage he didn't know he had rise within him. He thought of Nick's conversation the night before.

"I don't know where Nick went. I guess maybe he figured he wouldn't be a burden to us anymore and he'd travel on. We don't need to worry about him hurting any of us."

Stronger, he turned to face the crowd, faces worried fearful, or sympathetic. "Maybe you shouldn't trust me," he began, brushing sweaty hands down the sides of his dusty brown pants, his heart yammering in his chest. "I'm just Lee Connor from the Mississippi Orphanage. Haven't been anywhere or done anything with my life yet. I'm sure most of you are more experienced at a lot of things than me. But there's a couple of things I feel certain."

"What's that?" a voice called out.

Mark sneezed and Danny whispered, "Bless you." Lee smiled at the boys. "Kind of like what Danny just said.. God's blessed us and He's in control. Sure, maybe we have to go through hard times like Freddy stealing Nancy's wagon and supplies. But none of us got hurt or killed last night."

Greta's weary, grief-stricken face glanced up at him from a crate where she sat wrapped in her tattered white shawl.

"Eugene is the only one who's died on this trip." Surprisingly, Hanna helped him out. "And there's been plenty of times when any one of us could have been killed. But Trevor and Mr. Maxwell have guided us along so far. Lee's right, it is like somebody's looking out for us."

"Thank you, Hanna," Lee gave her a tentative smile, still aware there were more faces in the crowd who stared at him with tight lips and suspicious eyes. "And I guess there's something else I'm certain of too and that's what we can all accomplish together. Back at the orphanage, we didn't always have a lot. Sometimes there wasn't enough money to go around for our needs. But we knew if we stuck together and trusted one another, we'd somehow make it through. Last night, Nick reminded me of that fact. He said people can do anything with mutual trust. If we stay together and don't quit, we're going to make it to California. Freddy nor anybody else can stop us if we support each other and stay strong."

Shy at this outburst, Lee stopped, glancing down at his booted foot. *I've sure put my foot in my mouth this time. Telling all these older people how to live.*

A clap sounded. First one pair of hands clapping, then another and another and... to Lee's astonishment, he lifted his head to see everyone surrounding him clapping, smiling, and cheering him on.

"Thank you, Lee." Trevor smacked him on the back and reached up to ruffle his dusty blond hair as if he were a little boy. "You've reminded us all what we can do together, the reason we all joined a wagon train."

Mrs. Templeton gave him a smile from her usual dour face. "Young man, I've got a tad of maple syrup left and some hoe cakes from breakfast. I say let's pass it around and all have something to eat before we hit the trail."

"We've got bacon!" Nancy shouted. "It's the last, but we'll share."

"I've got a pot of beans on," Greta spoke up in a shy voice, seeming to notice someone other than herself for the first time since Eugene died. "Hanna and me'd be glad to share it."

Several other people crowded up with offers of food, and Mr. Morison admitted to having enough real coffee left for a pot or two. "By reason of a celebration," he mumbled as he clapped Lee on the back, "for getting to Fort Laramie sometime today."

Excitement filled the camp as everyone hurried around, gathering their offerings for the communal breakfast. Tin plates and cups clattered, women chattered like gossipy birds and the children ran around getting in everyone's way. As everyone kept piling food on his plate, Lee looked around at his new family.

Trevor came up to clasp him on the shoulder. "Maybe you should think of joining me one day as a trail boss or a scout, Lee. I could use a good man like you along. You've got a sensible head and you're good about making people trust you."

"Thanks for the offer," Lee blushed at the compliment. "but I guess I best keep my plan to get me and Danny to California."

Trevor shrugged in a good-natured fashion and walked away.

Me, Danny and... Lee looked at Nancy, in that silly faded dress of Josie's. *Maybe it's time I learned Nancy's story, now that she's my responsibility too.*

Chapter Twenty-Four

Fort Laramie

Wyoming

"We made it!" Danny shouted, overjoyed at seeing the fort before them. Lee didn't have the heart to tell him what Trevor had said long ago. *We're only a third of the way to California and most of my money and supplies are gone.*

Walking beside the wagon with Danny, Nancy pulled a straw hat of Josie's over her brown braid. "I wonder if we'll see Freddy here," she asked in a quiet voice. "Although I guess my wagon is long gone. And Beauty." She sighed in such a mournful way, Lee's heart clenched for her loss.

Me and Danny might not have much, but Nancy has nothing. Trying to lighten the mood, he snapped the reins and said, Well, I guess it's a good thing you didn't put your shoes in the wagon. So, you don't have to walk barefoot."

"Ha!" Nancy tried to joke back but Lee heard the hurt she tried to hide. "Got shoes, a Colt, a couple of pans and a torn nightgown. I'm sure all set for a thousand-mile journey."

Danny, hopping along like a jackrabbit, grabbed Nancy's hand. "You got me an' Lee too. We can be a family."

Nancy flushed under the straw hat, and Lee thought he saw her swallow. But her eyes stared at the trail before her feet.

The wagon, pulled by Charlie, the ox, lumbered toward the fort behind several others. *God sure knew what He was doing when he left Charlie beside the trail, now that Cletus is gone.*

175

Once again, he thought of Nick. *Someone's got us in the palm of his hand for certain.*

Even the animals seemed to sense the excitement o. something new and stepped livelier. James had a tussle with his mules, who took that opportunity to start nipping one another. "Whoa, now! Whoa!" He shouted to the two boys skipping along, "You critters stop that! Danny, you and Mark stay clear of those beasts, you hear!"

The fort wasn't quitethe wooden and gated building Lee had imagined. A large adobe walled structure, it wa. surrounded by officer's and soldier's quarters, a stable bakehouse, guardhouse, and powder magazine. There were no walls and the whole stood on a stark, treeless plain. Jus past the fort, Lee could see several encampments of wagons beside the Laramie River. It was hard from this distance to see if any of them were Nancy's.

Trevor rode up beside them, an eager glint in his travel-weary eyes, and the curve of a smile on his leather-tanned cheeks. "We'll camp over near the river. Everyone's going to circle around—you go after Hanna and Greta. We'll set up camp before we go into the sutler's store."

Lee kept his eyes open to see if he could spot Cletus o. Beauty. Having just Charlie, the ox, pull his wagon had been rough. He'd need another ox or mule to go the distance through the mountains. *And how am I going to pay for that.* The sudden weight of his responsibilities pressed harder on him. Almost as if he heard Nick beside him, the word calmed him down. "Trust."

It was probably the fastest they'd ever made camp. Everyone—except Greta—was eager to get out and explore the fort. "You all go on," Hanna whispered when Lee stopped to see if Greta wanted to come, "I went through all her supplies and added in mine." Hanna had just been traveling on a horse and pulling a pack mule for supplies. "Here's the money I have." She handed Lee a small leather pouch. "It ain't much but I figure we have to pool everything we have like you said this morning. Greta's not got much cash, but I made a list of her food and supplies. I tried to talk to her, but she don't much care right now. Still, she's got to get to California somehow. As near as I can figure, her and Eugene got land already paid for out there."

"Thank you, I'll try to make it go as far as I can." He took the pouch with a grateful heart.

"And—I figure since I'm pulling Greta's wagon, I won't need the horse and mule. So, Lee, you and Trevor decide if you want to trade them for something else or sell them."

Another blessing!

"I'm probably going to need another ox," he said, "especially if we don't find Nancy's wagon. I'm going to have to carry more supplies."

"Then do it." Hanna tugged one of Greta's shawls around her thin shoulders. "I trust you and Trevor to do what's best."

Lee couldn't deny it was an awesome responsibility, a load he didn't quite feel he could carry. *I'm glad Trevor's here too.*

The fort's store had more supplies than any of them had seen in months. Shelves groaned under fabric, boxes of ammunition, tinned foods, and every imaginable thing a person could need. Tin buckets and iron skillets hung from pegs; barrels of provisions lined the floors. Straw brooms and shovels stood at attention in a wooden box. A tangy, vinegary twang of pickles in brine and an earthy scent of fresh dug potatoes filled Lee's nose. An enormous pile of fur pelts was stacked Danny-high in one corner giving off its own pungent aroma.

"Look, Lee," Danny tugged his arm. "Licorice!"

Lee didn't have the heart to tell Danny their pennies were better spent on other supplies. Maybe the heavy-set, dark-bearded man behind the wooden counter understood his hesitation.

"Name's Bradford Cleet, I run this here general store. Whereabouts you from, young man?"

"Mississippi," Lee answered. "I'm Lee Connors and this is my brother, Danny."

The shopkeeper winked and drew a length of the dark candy from a glass jar to hand to Danny. "Welcome to Fort Laramie, Danny Connor."

Danny waited for Lee's nod before he accepted the sweet treat.

"Guess you'll want to stock up on supplies before you hit the mountains. Where you headed?"

"California," Lee answered, staring at a list of prices the man had written and stuck up on a heavy board plaque. Trevor had told him prices would be almost triple here. Even with the addition of Hanna and Greta's money, they'd be hard-pressed to buy enough food to get them the rest of the way to California. *I'm buying for five mouths now.*

"You'll need a lot of supplies to go that distance," Mr. Cleet said as he pushed back a lock of dark hair that dropped in front of his eyes. "You got a list?"

"Not yet, we're just looking around tonight. We're staying over a few days to get the wagons mended and buy more livestock. I know we'll need more cornmeal, probably bacon..."

"Bacon's sold out. Got salt pork I can let you have it but it's going fast too. We only get in extra supplies for the wagon trains a few months of the year. You all are coming in later than most."

"Yes, I know," Lee spent a few more minutes talking to Mr. Cleet before he walked out onto the wooden porch. Trevor hurried up from the stock pens. "I priced a couple of oxen we can have in a trade for Nancy's horse and mule. If you're willing, I'd say let's get them. I talked to some of the people who've come in the last week. They said Freddy Scott was here. Sold your horse to some folks going back East. They said he stocked her wagon and went on toward the gold fields."

There went that hope. Lee knew he'd have to put whatever supplies they needed into his wagon.

"Trevor, I've seen into the Richards' wagon, they haven't got much. You know how they are about charity. Can you think of any way we can get them the cash to buy more supplies?"

Trevor glanced around and got a thoughtful look on his face. "Well, I have heard of people who find work here for a few days. You might ask around. We can't camp long, or we'll be put behind, but maybe you could barter for some goods. James too."

"That's a thought." Lee turned and hurried back into Mr. Cleet's store.

"I wonder if you have any work you need done," Lee asked. "We're only going to stay a few days, but I need supplies and I'm short on cash."

"You got any carpenter skills, boy?"

"Yes, sir."

"Sure enough?" The man led Lee to a storeroom in the back of the building. "I need shelves put up in here and the supplies stocked up. Got no help most of the time and can't take the time to put up shelves. If you do it I can pay…"

Lee shook his head. "If you don't mind, I'd rather trade for supplies."

"That works fine too."

Lee looked and thought he could do it, but he'd probably need help. "I have a friend too. He needs to restock his supplies."

"Where is this friend?"

Lee pointed outside where James stood on the wooden porch, waiting to see if he'd be accepted into the store. The older man glanced back over his shoulder once or twice; Erica's overripe-pear shape seemed to have thickened, and she was moving more carefully. James hovered protectively around her whenever the trail allowed. "Hm—you vouch for him?" Mr. Cleet asked. "He's not a runaway slave, is he? Had his kind in here before."

It was probably useless to point out to this hard-faced stranger that the war had ended, and the slaves had been freed three years ago. "James is a free man. He has papers. But even if he didn't, I'd trust him with my life. In fact, I have more than once on this trip."

The man lifted a hamhock-sized hand and a lopsided grin split his bearded face. "Don't start the war all over again, son. I trust you. Let's see what kind of job you do before I judge. Paid a king's ransom to have boards hauled in for building— you build my shelves and I'll stock your wagons."

Lee smiled and then thought of Nancy, who would also need supplies.

"Another thing... could you use a woman to dust and clean up in here for a few days?" He stared pointedly at the cobwebs wafting from the ceiling and the mud spattered on the wooden floorboards. Dust was so thick on some of the goods, Lee knew he could write his name.

"Son, you drive a hard bargain." The man's grizzled face cracked a smile. "Still, you got a way about you makes me glad to help you."

***

Still wearing Josie's borrowed dress, Nancy waited for Lee and the others to come back to camp. She had walked around the fort with Josie and Mark, trying to figure out what to do.

My wagon's gone. My money. My clothes. I have nothing.

"Now, you don't worry about any of that," Josie said as they walked along, ignoring the soldiers who eyed Nancy's tangle of dark curls and delicate face. One took the liberty of giving her a bold wink while another laughed at Nancy's flush of embarrassment. "What I've got, you've got. Me an' Mark aren't so crowded you can't ride with us. And once we get to California, I'm sure you and Lee will be setting up house once you get married. Your beloved's not gonna let you starve on the trail."

Married! Of course, she still thinks Lee and I are betrothed.

Nancy was too upset to keep walking around the fort. She excused herself and hurried back to camp.

"Nancy, wait up!" She turned to see Lee, a jubilant look on his face crossing the bare ground toward her.

"You've found my wagon?"

"Oh." His face fell as if he hadn't realized what she'd think then he looked embarrassed. "No, I didn't. Trevor heard that Freddy was here and took it on west. I'm sorry. We didn't find Beauty either."

Nancy wanted to cry but she blinked hard to keep her emotions inside.

"But, Nancy, I have some good news." He told her about asking for work at the general store. "He said if you're willing to do some cleaning, he'd barter you for fabric and supplies whatever you need. Me and Danny can find room for your supplies too."

This time, Nancy couldn't keep the tears—tears of joy—from falling. *I almost wish he were my betrothed.*

Chapter Twenty-Five

Freddy Scott snorted in disgust and pushed the tip of his snakeskin boot toward the campfire. He nudged a stick of wood—very high-priced sticks of wood he'd bought in Ft. Laramie—back into the glowing fire. An iron spider sat over the coals, a delicious scent of beef stew promising a meal worthy of a king before long. He should be happy, but the emotion simmering in his heart was rage.

Nancy should be mine.

The more he'd thought of that night in Nancy's wagon, the angrier he became at not making her his own. Who would have thought a sweet, delicate little chit like her could use a gun to such advantage? Despite his desire, Freddy knew better than to argue with a Colt held in a trembling hand toward his heart.

As it was, she'd managed to hit Vince in the leg, and he'd had to be left behind when he bled out. *One disaster after another!*

So many times before, Freddy had been on the trail and he'd never had the misfortunes that befell him this time. Losing his wagon and all his merchandise—-thousands of dollars in potential profits gone up in smoke. He'd managed to sell Lee's horse to a couple going back east. Beauty, Nancy's horse, went lame from Spence's hard driving the night they stole her wagon. They'd managed to let her limp into the fort and brought her along, but Freddy didn't think she'd last the night. Someone would have to put the animal out of her misery before sunset.

Although he'd taken Nancy's wagon and dwindling number of supplies and bought more after selling Cletus, Freddy still felt as if he'd been cheated. Surprisingly, Nancy's strongbox had held less money than he'd expected her to have. He'd assumed from her wagon and supplies that she'd been set up by someone with money.

One setback after another! Stealing her wagon only got me ahead another few miles. It comes nowhere near replacing what I've lost! And now I'm saddled with a lot of weaklings.

Despite having led off part of Trevor's wagon train, he'd only managed to keep Spence and one other wagon together. The rest of the complainers had joined another party going out of Ft. Laramie, several others had decided to winter over near the fort. *So, it's me, Spence, the Kelsey's and another drifter we picked up at the fort.* Hardly enough people to make a stand against Trevor and Lee—if he decided to go that route.

She's beautiful. Staring into the orange red glow of the campfire, Freddy sighed. He had a wife back in Arkansas, but she'd grown old and fat from too many children. Freddy cared not a whit for her anymore. He seldom bothered to send any of his money back to help support her or his growing brood of offspring. Why should he? Hadn't her father conned him into marrying the girl years ago? Let him support her.

I want Nancy. As he stared into the fire, pondering the desire raging inside him, he realized it wasn't just to get back at Lee. He wanted Nancy because she was fresh, unsoiled— not like Hanna. Who knew how many men she'd allowed to touch her? He could tell Nancy had never been with a man- he would be the first. The thought excited him in a way he hadn't felt in a long time. He would have to find a way to make it happen. Trevor's train should be about a week behind him by now.

Biting off the tip of a pungent cigar, Freddy lit it and took a long, satisfying draw, and blew out the smoke. He stared off at Nancy's wagon, now filled with more supplies he could sel along the way. He'd sold most of the tools, seed and other farming supplies she'd carried at the fort. What did he need with all that? He'd kept the food he needed and supplemented it with the money from Cletus. Fine Belgian or not, he'd managed to ask more than the animal must have been worth. Desperate people always paid more.

Where had Nancy come from? It was still a mystery. Had she come from a wealthy family who wanted to get rid of her for some reason? She told Trevor she'd had an uncle who vanished on the trail. Was that true? Or might there be a wealthy family somewhere who would pay a handsome ransom to get her back. If not a family, would Lee?

Spence came to squat by the fire and dish out a tin plate of the stew. "Boss?" He'd begun to call Freddy that and Freddy found he enjoyed it. "That mare of Nancy's is on her last legs. I don't think she'll make it through the night. Some are like that—if you ride them too hard, they don't last. You want me to put her out of her misery?"

"Yes, fine. After she's dead, chop off the head."

Spence sputtered out a mouthful of stew. "What?"

"Chop off the head. I want to leave a message for someone."

***

"I sure do wish we could have stayed at the fort," Danny lamented as he trudged along beside Lee's wagon. Nancy had gotten Greta to walk today and the two of them were further back, chatting with Josie as she drove her wagon along. Mark darted back and forth, running ahead and back. He came up panting, his words coming out in a jumbled huff.

"Hey, Lee, g-guess w-what I seen just now up? It's a horse's head. Just the head."

"A horse head!" Danny loved animals and had been almost desolate over the loss of Cletus. Each time they came across the dead or skeletal animal carcasses along the trail, he cried real tears. "Just a head? You're joshing."

"Ain't neither."

"Show me!"

"Don't get too close," Lee warned, although the boys were too excited to listen as they raced past his oxen team. He had heard while working at the fort how some trains recently had been decimated with cholera.

"You all be careful now," Mr. Cleet admonished as they started back on the trail. "I've heard word several trains were wiped out with cholera recently. Had a scout come limping in a week ago, barely alive, died a couple of hours later. Said his whole train died. We sent out some soldiers to bury them. Fifty-nine men, women and children."

No one knew what carried cholera, but Lee had heard it was often in tainted meat or water. One theory said animals drank foul water and passed on cholera. No one really knew for certain.

"You got to be careful of eating meat out on the trail," Mr. Cleet gave another warning. "I've heard when antelope and such get desperate, they'll eat poison hemlock. Know it's poison but don't care if they're starving. Once a person eats the meat, he's a goner. You got to be careful once you pass the fort. Folks want game but it's not always best to eat it."

The boys ran ahead and peered down at the dark blob on the dusty ground. Danny turned, a stricken look on his face, and hurried back, running in his funny lopsided way with his twisted leg. When he got closer to the wagon, Lee could see he'd been badly frightened. The little boy's face blanched so white his freckles stood out like nutmeg on his face. His lips moved but no words came out.

"Danny, what's wrong?" They'd seen a lot of dead and dying animals on the trail. While Danny got upset each time, he'd never been this frightened before.

Tears slipped from Danny's blue eyes, "Lee, I think..." He swallowed, trying not to cry, "I think It's Beauty. Just her head like somebody chopped it off like a chicken."

Lee glanced back around the side of his wagon. About half a mile behind, he could see Nancy and Greta walking along, Nancy swinging a straw hat without a care in the world. He noticed Trevor, riding his black stallion past the wagon in the rear. "Wave down Trevor and have him come up this way. Don't say anything to Nancy."

Danny nodded and took off to flag down Trevor. A few minutes later, Trevor rode up beside Lee's wagon. "What's wrong?"

"The boys found a horse's head up the trail. Danny says it's Beauty."

"Nancy's horse?"

"Yes—he said it looked like it was chopped off..."

"Stay here."

Lee tugged the oxen to a stop, still struggling to get this new team to obey his commands, while Trevor rode ahead. Mark had stayed beside the head and appeared to be explaining his find as Trevor dismounted and squatted beside the dark blob on the ground. Trevor spoke to Mark and the little boy came running back.

"Mr. Trevor says have you got a burlap sack so he can pu'
the head inside? An' he says us men got to keep quiet anc
not scare the women folk."

Despite the seriousness of the situation, Lee had to grin a'
the expression on Mark's dusty little face. At the cute way he
yanked up his pants and tried to stand like a man.

Lee turned on the wagon seat, reached into the back anc
shook their clothes from a burlap sack. He tossed it down tc
Mark. By then Nancy and Greta had walked up close to the
wagon. Danny followed with eyes downcast.

"What's going on?" Nancy asked.

"There's something dead on the trail," Lee answered
"Trevor said it's not something ladies should see." Whicl
sounded awful silly to him; the women had been walkin∂
along past carcasses and skeletal remains for weeks now
They'd seen more graves than probably filled the Mississipp
Cemetery back home.

Greta shuddered. "Another puir creature," she mumbled ir
the brogue she'd picked up from Eugene after years o
marriage. "I'd be glad not to look."

Lee saw a question in Nancy's eyes, but she too stayec
quietly while Trevor tied up the burlap sack and carried it of
the trail. Mark came back for a shovel, and with Danny's hel∣
they buried Beauty's head and covered the grave with rocks.

Later that night, after they'd set up camp and gotten a
buffalo chip fire going, Trevor sought Lee out while Nancy anc
Greta made supper. Motioning Lee out of hearing, he
whispered his concerns.

"Lee, I guess we both know that horse's head was a
message from Freddy. He's still around and wants revenge.
Trevor sighed. "I guess the best we can do is to keep guard

We'll all have to take turns. You, me, Mr. Morison, James, and Frankie Templeton. Two of us at a time."

They ate supper and despite the cool evening— no one felt much like having any entertainment, although it had turned out Frankie Templeton could play a mean fiddle—a talent he'd kept hidden for most of the trail. The children enjoyed dancing a jig and even Nancy, Hanna and Josie had been known to lift their skirts a bit and dance a few lively steps. Tonight, everyone was too tired. It wasn't long before everyone finished their meal of beans and hoe cake and crawled under the wagons to sleep.

Lee sat on watch by the campfire with the rifle on his lap. Mosquitoes were bad tonight, nipping at any exposed skin. The smoke from the fire should have kept them away, but they buzzed and flew in an annoying cloud. A strange moan came from out of the darkness. Then another. Alert, Lee sat up and slid the rifle into his hand.

From the other end of the camp, he heard an owl's call, which meant Trevor had heard it too and wanted to alert him to the threat of something... they weren't sure what.

More moaning, and then the blackness of the night was split by a woman's piercing scream.

Chapter Twenty-Six

Nancy jerked awake, startled out of sleep. A scream of anguished pain ripped through the night. Grunts and moans came from Richard's wagon which was camped next to Josie.

"Erica!"

Struggling off the pallet under Josie's wagon, Nancy pushed her tumble of dark hair out of her face. Since she'd started to sleep under the wagon, she never changed into a nightgown. It was easier to sleep in her dress, just loosening a tight sash or buttons. As she crawled out from beneath the wagon, tugging her skirt where it had twisted around her waist, she met Josie climbing from inside the wagon.

"Reckon it's Erica's time," she muttered around a yawn. "We best go see how we can help her. Ain't never known a man yet who's any good at birthing."

Nancy nodded, heart in her throat. She had no idea what happened when a woman had a baby, never known anyone who gave birth. Although her friend, Susie, had often talked about having babies she had no idea how they were born either. While Mama had told Nancy about her monthly, she hadn't given her more information about being a woman. It had never occurred to her until Josie whispered one day, "I'm worried about when Erica's time comes. I sure hope we're near California by then—but by her size she looks about ready to drop that baby any day now."

"What baby?" Nancy had asked. It had never occurred to her that Erica was carrying a baby. She had wondered why Erica seemed to grow stouter and rounder while the rest of them shriveled to skin and bones. If she thought at all, she knew Erica ate very little, rejecting a lot of what she did eat and putting it down to a "sensitive" stomach. It had worried

Nancy that maybe Erica had some strange ailment. Having a baby had never entered her imagination. She had never seen a woman before she gave birth, never known how a woman's stomach rounded.

"Land sakes, child," Josie had looked at her in shock. "Didn't your mama ever tell you how a baby gets inside the mama and how it's birthed?"

Ashamed, although she couldn't begin to explain why, Nancy flushed and shook her head. One day as they walked along alone, Josie and Greta told her the facts of life. Information that startled Nancy so much she couldn't begin to understand it. *Was that what Mr. Morgan would have wanted if she married him?* The idea was frightening. Nancy couldn't begin to feel anything but revulsion. Especially when Josie told her what Freddy had probably wanted to do when he jumped into her wagon.

Nancy found the courage to ask Josie what a "soiled dove" really was and found herself shocked into silence. *How could a woman be so bold?*

She'd known there were "wicked" women, Uncle had told her so often enough—and those horrible names he called her! Although Nancy wanted to ask questions, embarrassment kept her from uttering a word to the two older women. *Does Lee know all about this too?* Nancy flushed so red her skin warmed hotly.

"Nancy," Josie grumbled, "come along now. First, get some clean cloths out of my clothes trunk, but don't wake Mark. That's all we need is that child in the way. Going to be a long enough night as it is."

Just then Lee and Trevor came up, both were armed from sitting up keeping watch. "Erica's time?" Trevor asked Josie.

Josie nodded.

Several others had heard Erica's screams and moans. Mr. Morison, dressed in long, red flannels, walked up barefooted. "What's the trouble?"

"Woman giving birth," Trevor said in a terse way.

Mr. Morison grunted and mumbled, "Should have gone on with Freddy. Now we're going to be slowed down more, Smith. I knew those two were trouble from the get-go."

"Go on back to your wagon," Trevor snapped. "You're standing guard in another hour."

The man grumbled but walked slowly away, stopping to pass the word to the Templetons peeking from the cover of their wagon. Nancy followed Josie, noticing how Lee looked at the wagon as if wondering what was going on too. *Maybe he's as dumb as me about such things.* The idea gave Nancy courage as she did as Josie asked and then climbed into the Richards' wagon to find Erica lying on a pallet, writhing in pain. Wearing a white nightgown, her dark skin shimmering with sweat, she moaned and twisted from side to side, holding the blanket between white-knuckled fingers.

James stood nearby twisting his hands together. When Josie climbed in, his face showed relief and he was quick to follow Josie's orders. "James, you get outside and build up a good, hot fire. Going to need some boiling water and scissors, maybe a clean length of thread. Be sure and pass them scissors through the fire first to clean 'em."

As he eased past Nancy, James' face wore a curious expression, but he managed a trembling smile just as Erica shrieked again.

"G-give me something to bite," Erica moaned, "so's I don't scare the little ones."

"Nancy! Find me that wooden spoon she uses in her cooking pot."

After Nancy had found the spoon, handed it to Josie and watched Erica clench it between her teeth, she stood nearby waiting for more commands, terrified at what she might see. Birthing a baby sure looked like painful, long-drawn-out toil.

Excruciating hours later, to Nancy's immense shock, Erica's baby slid into the world all bloody and wet. The little morsel dropped into Josie's hands. "It's a girl," Josie said, "looks healthy too."

Erica reached up for the baby after Josie cleaned her off and swaddled her in a blanket. She was sweating and tired, and her hands trembled with exhaustion. But Nancy had never seen a woman look so triumphant. "Jorja, me and James agreed. We're going to name her after where her grandparents was slaves—Georgia. Only we're gonna spell it different since she's born free."

***

Mile after mile after mile. Lee sighed as he unyoked the oxen he'd bought in Fort Laramie. A few days back, one of Greta's oxen had toppled over and died. He'd had to hitch Charlie, his old ox, to help carry Hanna and Greta's wagon further along.

Following the California Trail and avoiding the disasters that had befallen the Donner Party and others who had tried to cross the Great Salt Desert, Trevor had led them through something called the South Pass.

"We'll travel across Idaho and head on into Nevada Territory," he'd told them all around an evening campfire a few nights past. "It means we won't be near Fort Bridger, so we're going to have to buckle down on food and water. I don't like to ration water, but we need to be sparing. It's going to be miles before we cross the Humboldt."

People had grumbled, including the Morison's. It had been a long time since they'd all shared a meal before arriving in Fort Laramie. Despite Lee's hopes they could continue sharing and trusting one another, each mile led many of them to become tighter and greedier, less sharing with their supplies. While Lee tried to spare as much as he could, he knew Danny must come first in his responsibility, then Nancy. His supplies and those he'd helped Nancy earn at the fort were slowly diminishing.

"People are upset about the Richards," Trevor told Lee the night before. "The baby is keeping everyone awake at nights crying. James said Erica doesn't have enough milk to nurse the baby so it's colicky. I'm going to suggest they park their wagon off a way from the rest. We need to get some sleep if we want to keep moving ahead. I wish we could have rested awhile after Erica gave birth, but well... best to keep moving."

Lee knew what Trevor didn't want to say. The threat from Freddy Scott was all too real. One afternoon, they'd come upon a couple sitting beside the trail. Each of them had a small knapsack and a canteen.

"Man stole our wagon and our team," a tall, rawboned farmer said, "so me and the missus are done, going back east. Lost near about everything but some food he let us keep and some water."

"You're welcome to travel along with us," Trevor told them after asking them a few questions. No doubt the robber had been Freddy and a few others.

"Thankee kindly for the offer, but no siree. Wish I'd never left Missouri and that's a sad fact," the man said. The woman, eyes staring blankly at the world around her, neve uttered a word. When the man started to walk east, the soles of his hard-worn boots flapping, she trudged along behind him.

It was not long after that Ted Maxwell came racing back into camp from a scouting mission. "Antelope! I saw four or five hidden in a draw up ahead. Some of you men grab your rifles and come along! We can have fresh game for supper!"

Lee reached for the Henry until Trevor hurried up to stand beside him, "Lee, let Frankie and Mr. Morison go. I really need you to help with the axle on Greta's wagon. If she loses that wheel, we're in worse shape out here. We can't afford to lose more time."

Although he ached to grab his rifle and hunt, Lee did as Trevor asked. *We haven't had fresh game in over a month, I sure hope they shoot something.*

Chapter Twenty-Seven

"I got more children! I say I should get a bigger share!"

Nancy, rinsing out two of little Jorja's cloth gowns in a scant few inches of water, heard the shouts as she stood in the shade of her wagon. A few minutes earlier, she'd heard the men come riding back from their hunting expedition. Thrilled at the idea of fresh game – meat!- she peeked out to see they'd managed to kill one small antelope.

"That's a poor excuse for a hunting party," Josie said as she took Jorga's gowns to drape over the wagon wheel. "Best just chop it up and mix it in with a pot of beans so we all get a bite."

"Roasted venison sounds tasty to me," Nancy answered.

"We share!" Ted Maxwell hollered back. "Everyone gets a share, or no one does. I'm the one who shot it."

Trevor and Lee hurried into the fray. James Richards was there, maybe eager to get a portion for Erica. Although Nancy wouldn't admit it to anyone, little Jorga's incessant crying had gotten on her nerves plenty too. She'd taken to putting wads of cloth in her ears so she could sleep at night. It must be a hundred times worse for Erica, listening to the baby cry and unable to help her.

A couple of the men's faces grew red and angrier. Frankie Templeton jumped toward Mr. Morison's older son, Joe, and punched him. "I'm not sharing! My Ma needs nourishment!"

Startled, Nancy stepped back toward Josie. "What's happening? I don't understand why we can't share."

"They're worried," Josie answered, "I'm going to find Mark and Danny and keep them away from this. It's like a pack of dogs fighting over a bone. Sure pray we don't come to that."

Unsure what to do or where to go, Nancy waited by the wagon as the crowd grew angrier and louder. Suddenly, a gun retort shattered the air and everyone went silent. Trevor jumped on a rock, gun pointed toward the searing blue of the sky, and said in a steady, unyielding voice. "We are going to roast this venison and everyone who wants it gets a share! The first person who tries to take more than his share will be shot! We aren't going to fight over food out here. I'm the wagon master and I say what goes!"

***

The scent of the roasting venison filled the camp with its enticing aroma. Nancy could hardly wait to taste the meat. Hunger pangs gnawed her stomach, and she could have chewed on dried fruit or hardtack, but she wanted to wait for the meat. Over her campfire, she stirred a pot of beans and mixed up another round of cornbread. Both would taste good with the meat.

Lee walked up, a worried frown on his face. "Where's Danny?"

"He went for a walk with Josie and Mark until supper." Nancy gave the beans a swift stir and moved the cast iron skillet to the edge of the fire. "I sure will be glad when the meat's done. It smells so good."

"Nancy."

She looked up at the quiet tone of his voice. "Nancy, don't eat the meat. I can't tell you why, but I've got a bad feeling about it. I'm not going to let Danny eat it either."

"Why?"

Although she'd discovered along the trail she could depend on Lee, he often did things she couldn't understand, for reasons that were his own. Josie had said men did things different than women, but Nancy didn't think that was a good enough explanation. Look at Uncle, he sure enough never had a good reason for most of what he did. Thinking of Uncle put some gumption into her spine. "You aren't my boss. I guess I can eat it if I want to."

Lee's green eyes stared at her with sadness. "That's true, but I'm asking you not to because I... I care for you, Nancy. The storekeeper at the fort told me there's a lot of cholera and disease out here. There's even been talk about anthrax out here killing some of the native tribes. People die from eating tainted meat. I don't want you to be one of them."

"So why is anybody eating it?" But she couldn't blame the rest of the travelers. That savory scent was driving her wild, and only her tentative trust in Lee made her place any weight on his words at all.

"I passed on what the shopkeeper told me to all of 'em," he answered. "Can't hold a gun on people and demand they not eat, I just..." He grimaced down at his shoes. "It just don't feel safe."

He cares for me. A thrill shot through Nancy and her heart gave a funny skip-hop.

"All right, Lee. We can eat these beans and cornbread. I don't need venison."

Danny came up in time for supper. The little boy argued as the scent of roasting meat, spinning over a spit, perfumed the camp site. "How come we can't eat meat? Everybody else is eating it. Even Miz Josie let Mark have some. He said it tasted fine."

"I'm not eating it, Danny," Nancy said as she dunked an edge of cornbread in her plate of beans. "Josie isn't either. I asked her."

Although the little boy mumbled under his breath, he ate his beans and then went off to check on the oxen. "Move the pickets so they can graze tonight," Lee reminded him.

Dusk came on and night sounds filled the camp. Various fires glowed in the dark. Nancy used a precious few inches of water to wipe off the tin plates they'd used. Then, because Lee sat by the fire on a wooden crate, she settled down on a chair they'd found earlier on the trail. For some reason, Mark and Danny thought that busted chair, the slats all punched to splinters in the back, was the funniest thing. They'd dragged it along to present to Josie earlier.

"How did you get left alone on the trail, Nancy?"

The question, coming out of the dusk, startled Nancy. It had been so many months since she'd thought of that lonesome, scary time. Like she'd been another Nancy back then. "My uncle left me there. After Mama died, he decided we'd go out to California so he could pan for gold. I didn't want to go but didn't have no choice."

"I'm sorry. But how'd he come to just leave you there? Were you attacked or robbed?"

"No," Nancy looked at Lee's face, softened by the firelight. *I should tell him about Mr. Morgan.* But what did it matter now? Mr. Morgan's one cherished letter had been stolen in her wagon, probably still sewn inside her pin cushion buried in the sawdust. *I will never meet Mr. Morgan in person.* Somehow, the thought didn't ache as it once might have. "My uncle..." Maybe it was the night and the way they sat beside the campfire, just the two of them. Nancy opened her mouth and the words poured out to Lee's sympathetic ear. She told him about Uncle, his fierce ways, how mama had died, how she never had friends or a beau.

Lee sat and listened. He didn't judge or condemn. Nancy had never had anyone listen as he did that night, not even Greta or Josie. Not even Mama had ever listened and let her talk without judging. After she'd confessed everything about writing to Mr. Morgan, because Suzie told her it would be a way to get away, he was silent for so long that Nancy worried.

Maybe he thought she was a wanton woman too—although now that she'd had Josie explain just what such a woman did, Nancy knew she had never done any of that with a man. Uncle had no right to call her such names.

"I'm sorry, Nancy. Looks like you had no choice but to write to that man to get away. Do you still want to look him up once we get to California?"

"No. Josie says you have to really love someone to give him your heart and I don't think I've got those kinds of feelings for him. Not anymore. Not since I've known..." She was too shy to complete the sentence and say the word. *You.*

A small grin came across Lee's face as if he understood anyway. He stood and came over to her. "Nancy, I know the last time I didn't ask and you got your dander up, but well, kind of feel like I'd like to kiss you again. If you reckon you wouldn't mind."

"I don't think I'd mind at all."

As his lips pressed down on hers, so sweet and gentle, Nancy felt a thrill inside she'd never felt before. *Love?* Lee bent his head and kissed her again, firmer and surer this time. Nancy wanted to press herself against his chest and stay there forever.

"Hey, Lee," Danny interrupted the moment and they jerked apart, "I put the oxen out, but Mrs. Greta says can you look at Charlie? He looks kind of poorly tonight."

Nancy touched her lips with the tips of her fingers, wishing Lee's lips were still pressed against hers.

Chapter Twenty-Eight

Lee didn't know what jolted him from a sound sleep. Half awake, he sat up on his pallet, rubbing sleep from his eyes. A moan, then someone retching. Groggy, tired in every bone of his body, he sat for a minute.

Blinking hard in the blackness of night, he heard a low plea. "Help, help me."

He crawled out from under the wagon, checking first on Danny as he did. The little boy slept heavy, curled in a gray army blanket, a small snore coming from his lips. There was more light than there should have been, and he stood up to see Nancy at the campfire, heating a pot full of water over the flames.

"Nancy. What are you doing?"

"Heating some water," she answered in a low voice. "We've got troubles."

"What's wrong?"

"Mark's sick, he woke up with a fever about an hour ago. I think a few others are sick too. Greta came by to say Hanna's been retching since midnight."

The meat! The ominous story the shopkeeper told him about burying fifty-nine people on a wagon train came back to haunt him.

"Yes, let me check on some of the others first."

Lee hurried to the end of the camp where Mr. Morison should be standing guard. It was no surprise to find the older man slumped on the ground, shivering and gasping for breath. "Mr. Morison!" Although he shook the man's shoulder, he couldn't seem to rouse him. "Joe!" He called toward their wagon. "Bring a lantern, your father is ill."

Joe Morison half fell from the wagon, sweat pouring from his forehead, his face flushed. "I'm sick too, I can't..." he fell to the ground, gagging.

Climbing to look inside the wagon, Lee could tell Mrs. Morison looked to be alive but ill too. The other children were crouched over a pallet, retching..

Lee hurried to where he'd seen Trevor lay his pallet, only to find it empty and unslept on. A few feet away, Trevor knelt beside Tad Maxwell's pallet, holding a tin cup of water to the man's trembling lips. Tad could barely hold up a shaky hand and the water spilled all down his chin. "Is he ill too?"

Trevor nodded. "Looks like anyone who ate the meat is sick, it must have been tainted somehow."

"What can we do?"

"The best we can," Trevor clenched his jaw and reached out to help Tad hold the tin cup. "Without knowing what was wrong with the meat, we can't really treat it. Could be anything—cholera, anthrax, the antelope could have eaten poison hemlock or any other poison thing. Give anyone who's sick water and try to keep them warm. Other than that, I don't know."

Lee thought of Mrs. Ewell's careful list of receipts for illness. Although he'd used a few remedies for Danny and others on the trail, he had no idea what to do about this mysterious sickness. He built a fire, heated water, and boiled some herbs Greta gave him to make tea. He went from person to person, trying to keep them warm or have them drink some tea. An hour later, Ted Maxwell breathed his last. Trevor, visibly shaken, covered his friend's face with a blanket.

They didn't have time to grieve because Nancy hurried up. "Lee, Mark's in a bad way. He can't hardly breathe."

Although there was nothing he could think to do, Lee hurried to where Josie sat beside the campfire, Mark wrapped in a blanket on her lap.

"Mark, you don't feel good?"

The little boy shook his head, so weak that drool rolled out his mouth. "M-my belly hurts awful bad."

"I shoulda never let him eat that meat," Josie mourned, "but I wanted to make him stronger, and I thought he needed it. I let him have my share."

"Mark," Nancy held out a spoon, "this is medicine Greta gave me. Can you try to sip a little?" To Lee she said, "It's paregoric, maybe it will help."

The little boy twisted his face away from the bitter brew after it touched his lips. "It's nasty."

"C'mon, Mark," Lee encouraged as he took the spoon from her hand. "Just a sip."

He'd just turned when he heard Nancy's sharp intake of breath and muffled scream. Turning, he saw a shape come from out of the darkness and the sound of several horses.

Freddy!

Freddy stood with his arm clenched around Nancy's middle and the other holding Lee's Henry rifle. Too late, Lee realized he'd left the rifle leaning against the wagon wheel earlier in the night. Behind Freddy, Spence and several other mean-looking men glared from their saddles, the horses snorting and stamping. It looked like Freddy had found a few more "outlaws" to join him in his devilment.

"Let her go," Lee stood and tried to look stern, although his throat balled tight with fear.

"Or what?" Freddy chuckled, his features twisted in the campfire with a devilish look. In one hand, he waved the Henry and then tossed it up to Spence, astride a large black Morgan. "I'm taking Nancy with me and there's nothing you can do about it."

Lee clenched his fists, aware of James Richards close behind, Trevor moving forward—possibly armed. But Lee didn't have a scrap of thought to spare for the wagon master—he sensed this was something between him and Freddy.

Nancy's cornflower blue eyes beseeched him for rescue.

"Let her go." Trevor repeated and cocked his Colt.

Spence pointed Lee's rifle at Trevor. "Drop it."

Reluctantly, Trevor did.

Lee stepped forward. He'd seen the tiniest glint of metal beside the campfire. Another step forward and he could see what he'd hoped to see. Nancy's Colt! Ever since the night of Freddy's attack, she kept it close by. "Let her go, Freddy, or fight me fair and square."

"You're unarmed."

In one swift motion, Lee bent and grabbed up the Colt. "Not any more, I'm not!"

Freddy shoved Nancy aside and drew his Colt from the holster on his side. Lee heard guns cock from the men on horseback, but Freddy motioned them to stop. "No! This is my fight! A man against this boy who thinks he knows so much! Take out anyone who tries to help him."

"Count of three, Freddy?" Lee suggested.

Freddy ignored the request, spun the Colt up and pulled the trigger. The gun jammed!

"Kill him!" James hollered. A look of terror seized Freddy's face; he knew he was about to die.

Lee aimed Nancy's Colt but knew he could never take a man's life. Never had and never planned to unless necessary. Instead, he shot at the edge of Freddy's expensive snakeskin boots, taking off enough of Freddy's knee to burn like the devil but not to maim him for life. Blood spurted and the man hollered like a scalded pig!

Spence had raised his own weapon, but Lee stopped him with a careful shot that bore through the man's hat and sent it spinning off his head. "Give me back my rifle, and then the lot of you get. Don't come back."

Freddy, cursing, limped to his horse and managed after two attempts to climb into the saddle.

Behind Lee, Trevor, James and Frankie Templeton pointed their own weapons at the bandits. The men rode off, following Freddy.

As Lee turned to thank everyone, he saw Trevor collapse on the ground.

"Trevor!"

Chapter Twenty-Nine

It was the longest, hardest night Nancy had ever lived though. Even those horrible nights alone on the trail after Uncle left weren't as terrible as tending to the sick and dying.

Along about dawn, Mark Evans drew his last breath. Josie wouldn't give him up but kept holding the still, limp body on her lap.

"He's gone up to Heaven, Josie. Maybe he's meeting up with his pa and his brothers."

Danny sat there with a bewildered look on his face, silent tears dripping down his gaunt cheeks. "I was savin' a piece of licorice for when he felt better."

Josie put an arm across his shoulders, "He would have liked that." To Nancy she said, "I just want to hold him awhile longer. You best go check on some of the others."

Nancy went to Greta's wagon to check on Hanna. Despite all the women in the train gossiping about Hanna at the start, the last few months Hanna had proven her true worth helping Greta. They had even talked about going to McGregor's farm together once they reached California.

Hanna lay on a pallet beside the campfire, sweating with fever or shivering with chills. At Greta's insistence, she'd sip a few spoonfuls of water or tea, only to retch it up a second later. Greta sat faithfully by her side.

"How are you doing, Hanna?" Nancy asked.

"N-not so good. How's everybody else?"

Nancy didn't have the heart to tell her Mark and Ted Maxwell had died, or how many others were near death. "We're all just fine. Now you get better too, you hear."

When she left Hanna, Nancy went to find Lee putting another blanket over Trevor. "Isn't there anything we can do? Maybe if we had medicine or something?"

Trevor shivered on his pallet, despite the pile of blankets and buffalo robes Lee put on top of him. "There might be a doctor at the trading post. If you ride due west, Lee, there's a settlement up ahead at Genoa. Can't say you'll find a doctor but it's worth a try."

"I don't like to leave you here alone," Lee told Nancy as they walked away to discuss it. "What if Freddy comes back?"

"I don't think they will, and I have my Colt." She lifted her chin and despite the fear in her heart gave him a saucy grin. "I'm a pretty fair shot, if you'll remember."

"I remember." He gave her a deep, longing kiss and went to saddle a horse.

***

Genoa

Nevada Territory

It was late afternoon when Lee rode into a small valley. A sturdy wooden building with a weather worn sign announced "Trading Post". A smaller building had a garish, faded sign that read "*Picket's* Saloon". The tall, sturdy man running the trading post directed him to try the saloon.

"You ask the Lieutenant, he knows just about everyone around these parts," he said when Lee asked for a doctor.

Lee walked into the dim room that smelled of whiskey and stale tobacco. To his surprise, it was almost empty except for a lone man sitting at a table and another man washing glasses behind the bar. "I'm looking for the Lieutenant," he said, directing his gaze to the man at the bar. He nodded to the other man at the table, working on account books and drinking, strangely enough, a white mug of coffee.

"Excuse me, sir," Lee directed his question to the man at the table, "I'm trying to find a doctor for..."

The man looked up.

Thomas?

"Thomas?" There was no mistaking that devil-may-care glint in his warm, brown eyes or the slight tilt of his lips. He was older, more worn, his face wore deep furrows of worry and a strange scar marred the top of his forehead, but there could be no doubt. *I'd recognize him anywhere.*

"Do I know you?"

"It's Lee, Lee Connor from the Mississippi Orphanage."

"Lee? Little Lee?" Thomas jumped up so fast the wooden chair scooted back across the floor with a squeal. "Lee!" Thomas grabbed him in a fierce bear hug and lifted him off his feet. "What are you doing way out here in this godforsaken country? Harry, a cup of coffee for my friend here—unless you want something stronger. You must be of age now."

"Coffee's fine." After the past days, coffee was heavenly.

"Sit, tell me what you've been doing since I went off to join the army."

Lee drank coffee and told Thomas—Lieutenant Thomas Stevenson, he learned during the conversation—about the wagon train and the need for a doctor.

"Tainted meat?" Thomas grew thoughtful. "Could have been any number of things. Couple of tribes had trouble lately with antelope who grazed on poison hemlock. Well, no matter. Old Doc Burkhart is retired but he's been known to help folks out as the need comes. He's not far off."

Thomas stood with his take-charge air. "Harry, can you walk over and get Mrs. Thorndike to gather a few of the women in town to help out? Maybe come nurse the sick? My friend here says there's about twenty sick from tainted meat."

It didn't take long for Thomas to saddle a horse – a scrappy little quarter horse whose movements promised a good turn of speed— and set things in motion. The doctor would ride out as quickly as he could, along with some of the women from Genoa to help nurse the sick. As they rode back to the wagon train, Thomas talked and talked.

Lee didn't think he could ever get enough of listening to Thomas. When Thomas seemed to run out of words, Lee asked some questions of his own. "Why didn't you ever come back to the orphanage after the war?"

"Wasn't no reason," Thomas answered. "I got an honorable discharge and stayed on in Georgia to help during Reconstruction. After a year or so, I came out west to make my way in the world. I've got a fine ranch, built it up to over a thousand head of cattle now. In fact, I could use a man like you to help me build up my ranch. Maybe start one of your own."

"Well, I was set on going out to California."

"Why? Gold rush is just about played out. A man can't do better than to have his own spread here—plenty of room for a man to grow, raise a family."

"I'll think about it."

***

Over the next few weeks, Lee thought of Thomas' idea more than once. The doctor wasn't able to do a lot for the sick—no one really knew the cause of their illness—but he was able to save the two little Morison children and their older brother, Joe. Mrs. Templeton and Frankie were spared. Trevor recovered, although he looked as weak as a newborn kitten most days. It didn't stop him from making plans to head on out to California.

Greta nursed Hanna until the end. "I'm sorry now I ever spoke agin' her at the start," she told Lee and Nancy, "she ended up bein' a fine woman." They buried her in the small cemetery in Genoa. Greta insisted on having a marker carved for her grave. *Hanna Miller. A Good Woman.*

About a week later, they found Freddy Scott's body had been found along a nearby trail. Scuff marks and uprooted plants in the dry earth told the tale: an argument between Freddy and the "outlaws" that had led to the sutler's death.

Despite his distaste for the man, Lee saw to it that Freddy too got a decent burial and a marker. So many had died unmarked and unmourned along the trail, it just didn't feel right to leave a man for the coyotes and vultures. Trevor helped him send word back to Freddy's wife in Arkansas along with a small donation.

"I feel bad about Freddy," Lee told Trevor. "If he would have just gotten along with everyone, we'd have treated him better. His death seems so senseless. I feel like I'm to blame for shooting him."

ZACHARY MCCRAE

"Freddy made his own bad luck," Trevor said. "Don't ever regret taking a stand, Lee. If you do the right thing, God rewards that."

As the people recovered, Trevor announced his plan to continue with anyone who wanted to go west. The Templetons decided to go on and offered to take Greta with them. After Joe Morison buried his parents, he too decided to travel on. There was no doubt Josie would continue on to meet her older son, Matthew, in Coloma. To Lee's sorrow but not his surprise, she asked him around a campfire one night if he'd consider letting her adopt Danny.

"I know it's not right taking your brother from you, Lee," she said, "but since Mark died, I feel close to the little fellow. can give him a good life. My son, Matthew, he's near your age and a hard worker. Danny could visit you whenever you say."

Lee had put the idea to Danny. After all, it was his life. "always wanted a real Ma," Danny said, "and I think I'd like to go on with her. Mark was my friend an' I think he'd like to know I was taking care of his ma."

That left only Nancy.

"Nancy, I've been thinking," Lee said one night as they sat companionably beside the campfire. "I've decided I don't want to go on to California. My friend, Thomas, showed me a small parcel of land yesterday. If I work for him a couple of years, he will help me buy the land and enough cattle to start my own ranch. It seems like a sure thing."

Nancy gave a quiet, "Oh."

"If you're bound to go to California, maybe you'd like to travel along with Josie. You could have my wagon and the oxen. Maybe you can even find that Mr. Morgan you told me about... if you still think about him."

"Not so much," Nancy admitted, "anymore."

Those cornflower blue eyes stared at him and Lee thought of those stolen kisses, the way she pressed her small hands against his chest. "Or... I was thinking... I don't have a lot to offer right off, just my heart. But if you'd like to be my wife, Thomas says there's a circuit preacher comes through next week. We could be married if you..."

Her whispered, "yes, oh yes," told Lee all he needed to know.

***

Nancy wore a blue dress and carried a small bouquet of wildflowers Mrs. Thorndyke had given her. She held them in trembling hands as the preacher spoke the wedding vows over her and Lee.

Thomas stood beside Lee as his best man and Nancy had insisted that Josie stand with her before they left for California. Everyone from the wagon train crowded into the small saloon for a wedding dinner after the ceremony. There was roasted chicken—untainted, Harry the bartender had joked—fresh potatoes and butter, yeast rolls, all real treats. But everything tasted like sawdust through Nancy's nerves.

Later, after everyone had toasted them with apple cider, Mrs. Thorndyke led them to a spare room behind the saloon where they could stay until they moved to Thomas' ranch.

Being alone with Lee in that room, the warm glow of the lamplight shining in his green eyes, Nancy couldn't seem to stop trembling. When he took her in his arms, she wanted to weep from so many emotions surging in her heart at once— love, fear, uncertainty. Maybe he understood.

"What's wrong, Nancy? Are you sorry you married me?"

"Oh, no, no... I..." She pressed her face into the warm, sun-scented linen of his best blue shirt. "I wanted to marry you but I'm... scared. I've never been with a man before. I don' know..."

Nancy felt the smallest of chuckles against her cheek. He pulled her away so he could look down into her eyes. "You want to know a secret?" He whispered. When she nodded, he said, "I'm scared too. I've never been with a woman before."

"What should we do, Lee?" she whispered back, not sure why they weren't talking in normal voices.

"If you promise not to slap me," a grin transformed his face, that sweet gap between his teeth making her fall in love with him all over again, "I think we best start with a kiss."

"All right." She stood on tiptoe to reach up to press her lips to his, but it didn't matter. He scooped her up in his arms the skirt of her blue dress trailing along as he carried her to the white counterpane of the feather bed.

Epilogue

"Whoa!"

Nancy Conner pulled the shiny black fringed buggy to a stop beside the big, white framed house of home. As she often did, she sat just a minute staring in wonder at the wide, welcoming porch. Morning glory vines in pink and white climbed the trellis that shaded her favorite place to sit outdoors. White wicker furniture and a small table Lee had carved when they were first married sat in the shady refuge.

My favorite spot.

As always, Nancy took a minute to appreciate all that she'd been blessed with since that day long ago when Uncle abandoned her on the trail to California. *The happiest day of my life and I didn't know it then.* She had never heard what happened to Uncle, but she often wished he knew about her. *I'm not the terrible woman you thought me to be, Uncle.* Until Lee, she had never been with a man. Even today, ten years married and with two sons, Nancy could still feel a blush warm her cheeks when she thought of being with Lee, his strong arms wrapped around her, loving her.

"Mama?" Eight-year-old Thomas came running up to climb on the step of the buggy. "Did you bring me anything from town?"

"Did you do your chores?"

"Mama!" His voice dragged the word out in a teasing way, then he thought better of it. "I always do my chores. Papa says I'm the man of the house when he's gone. So, I did everything he said."

"Where is your Papa?"

"He and Mr. James went out to look at some of the cows in the south pasture. One of them stepped in a hole or something an' Mr. James said he could check. Papa said, if you said it's all right, me an' Nicky can go swimming in the creek after we did our chores."

Nancy smiled down at her blond-haired son, his sturdy little body and grinning face reminding her of his papa the day she'd first met him. Tommy's front teeth even had the same small gap as Lee. "I suppose that's fine. Did Nicky do his chores?"

"Yes, every single thing."

Nancy gathered her long, wine-red skirt and stepped out of the buggy, the letters she'd brought from town tucked against her bodice. "Help me carry in my packages and you can go swimming. And here's a treat," she handed him a small striped packet from the General Store in Genoa.

"Hard candy!"

"Only one piece until after supper," she reminded him as always, "share with Nicky."

"Yes, ma'am." Tommy raced into the house, dropped the packages on a table and hurried off calling, "Nicky! Mama said yes!"

***

Hurrying up to the big ranch house, Lee dusted off his brown pants, hitting his large, tan Stetson to sift out the trail dust. He'd left his Morgan at the barn where James offered to unharness both their animals.

"I'm glad we could get that cow fixed up," Lee said, "she's prized breeding stock. You sure know how to keep this ranch running, James. I don't know what I'd do without you."

James just gave him his usual gentle smile. He, Erica and their three children lived in a house a mile away. It wasn't as grand as the house Nancy had wanted, but the Richards were pleased with the one they planned and had built. Lee didn't know what he'd have done without James' and Thomas' experience and know-how to begin the ranch.

He walked into the dim quiet of the house and stopped to see if Nancy had brought the mail from town. *A letter from Trevor!*

Standing in the spacious hallway, he ripped open the envelope and read:

Dear Lee,

Just want you to know that I've decided to settle down and stay out here in California. Now that the railroad goes from the Atlantic to the Pacific, hardly anyone wants to make the trek across the country anymore. The whole country's got so overrun, it's not like those days when we went across, is it?

Lee stopped, remembering that long-ago wagon train and how young he'd been.

I'm settling down with a nice girl from Coloma, of all things. Danny's working at Peterson's livery nearby, and he's almost ready to take it over his ownself. Lee vowed to send Danny some money if he needed to buy out the business. Danny loved animals and had shown himself to be a quick study in caring for them. Despite the challenge his deformed leg had set him, Danny had never let it slow him down or keep him from doing anything he set his mind to.

"Oh, you found your letter!" Nancy came down the stairs, her dark hair tumbled across a sleep-flushed face. "I was so tired I laid down for a nap while the boys were swimming."

"Did they do their chores?" Lee asked, watching as she walked toward him. He gathered her in his arms and kissed her deeply, loving the fresh, lavender scent of her and the way she fit right into the space under his chin.

"Yes, they did," she mumbled against his chest, pressing her face into the warm linen shirt he wore. "You sir, smell like cow."

Lee chuckled and pulled away. "Cattle are our fortunes, dear wife. I love the smell of cow."

Nancy stepped away; her delicate nose crinkled. "I love it too but not on you. You need a bath."

"Soon," he promised. "Soon." He showed her the letter. "Trevor's doing good, and Danny's on his way to buying out Mr. Peterson's livery."

"Oh, yes, Josie wrote me a letter. Danny plans to write to you soon and let you know. He wants to ask a loan to buy out the business."

"He's my brother," Lee protested. "He doesn't need a loan."

"Josie doesn't think you should just give it to him. Maybe he needs to work for it."

Lee thought that over. "Well, I'll write to Josie and see what's in her mind, but I'd like to make a gift of the money to Danny. He's eighteen now—time he was thinking about making his own way in the world like I did. If all my neighbors hadn't given me a start, I'd never have been able to meet up with the wagon train."

Lee thought of those days long ago when he'd had to leave the orphanage with a gifted horse and wagon, and enough supplies to get him to California. *Was I really so young at eighteen?*

"I'll send Josie a letter tonight," Lee decided and at Nancy's insistence, went to take a bath. Later, after supper with the boys chattering about their days and Nancy filling him in on who she'd seen in town, Lee went to stand on the front porch. In the west, the sun had left just a faint orange yellow glow on the horizon. Night birds and insects chirped and sent out drowsy chatters.

So many years ago. Was it just ten when he'd set off from the Mississippi Orphanage? Lee stood on his front porch staring out at his land, his barns and corrals. The dark forms of thousands of cattle dotted the hills and pastures nearby. A mile away, through a stand of Eastern Cottonwoods, Lee saw the yellow glow of a lamp burning from James' kitchen window. Erica would be sitting up, feeding their youngest daughter, eight-month-old Betty.

Good friends, a good wife, my sons, and all this land. I'm truly blessed. Thank you, God.

"What are you thinking?" Nancy came up behind him and circled his waist with her arms. She pressed her face to his back and hugged him tightly.

"About time going by and way back when."

"It's too fine a night to be thinking so deep. Are you coming to bed soon?" She asked in a wistful voice, as if she couldn't wait for him to pull her close and wrap her in his strong, loving arms.

"Soon," he whispered. "There's something I need to do first." He leaned down to kiss her, thinking back to that first fumbling kiss when he'd pretended to be her betrothed to save her from Freddy's attention. He chuckled deep inside

"What are you laughing about?"

"Our first kiss."

"Oh, that!" Nancy backed away and circled to face him. " sure did smack you a good one."

"You sure did. But tell the truth…" He pressed his forehead down to hers and stared into her cornflower blue eyes, "you liked it didn't you?"

"Hm." Nancy pressed closer. "you'll never know. You come to bed soon and maybe I'll have a few more of those kisses stored up for you."

Before she could get away, Lee pulled her close and kissed her eagerly, hungrily before she pulled away with a beguiling smile. "I'll be up soon," he promised.

Lee went into the room where he kept his accounts and counted out the pay for his hired men. Nancy called it his "study", but Lee said it was just his writing and reading room. He sat down in a leather chair behind his big oak desk filled with cubbyholes where he kept account books, letter paper, bottles of ink and just about everything he needed to handle the business side of his ranch. On the top of the desk he found a small, scribbled note in Tommy's handwriting

Dear Papa, I did not rember to clen out my ponies stall like you tole me. I am sory. Pleze do not be to angry. Tommy.

Lee grinned. He had never felt the need to take a switch to either of his boys. As they grew, he tried to teach them to be honest and admit when they were wrong. Tommy would pay for his mistake by losing some of his free time tomorrow While Nicky went out to play, Tommy would be in his room sitting in a hard-backed chair to think about his misdeed When Danny visited, he called it a 'soft' punishment and kept the boys enthralled and horrified at Mr. Montgomery's usual mode of justice for misdeeds.

***

Mr. Montgomery. Standing on the porch, remembering back, Lee had thought of the orphanage director—Greg.

It felt strange to call him Greg, even in his thoughts—but the man would only be in his fifties now. At twenty-eight, Lee thought how ancient the man had seemed ten years ago. How heartbroken he'd been to leave the orphanage, the only home he'd ever known. At some point in the years between, though, Lee had realized Mr. Montgomery had done him a favor. If he hadn't forced him to leave, Lee would never have met Nancy.

He'd never have married and had Tommy and Nicky. He would never have met the Richards and Trevor or any other of his dear friends from the wagon train. Thomas never would have come back into his life. Once, when he'd been talking about it with Nancy, he'd realized a fact. The idea startled him because he'd never thought of it before.

I guess it's like a bird leaving the nest—if it doesn't leave, it doesn't live. Mr. Montgomery sent me off in life because he loved me. He cared enough to set me on my way.

After he'd settled the accounts and written a short few lines in his daily ledger, he pulled some foolscap from a drawer, a bottle of ink and a fresh pen nib. Then, he pulled the treasured daguerreotype from out of a drawer, faded and worn now from that long-ago rough wagon trip. He stared at the faces, a smile curving his lips. Dipping the pen in the ink, he stared down at the blank paper and then began to write:

Dear Mr. Montgomery,

I hope you will remember me, Lee Connor, because I certainly remember you. You were the father I never had and a big influence on my life. I've often thought of telling you how much I wanted to thank you for telling me I had to leave.

I know it wasn't your decision entirely, our lives were ruled by the board of directors on many occasions. But, I know now how much you wished I could stay on. Thank you for being strong enough to tell me I must make my own way in the world. I know you hoped I'd stay close by in Natchez, maybe even one day help with the other orphans – but the call West just beckoned too hard. You were right to send me off.

Lee went on to describe his ranch and how he would be enclosing a regular donation to the orphanage. He'd sent anonymous amounts in the past, but now he wanted Mr. Montgomery to be able to count on those donations. If there were orphans to house and feed, Lee knew Mr. Montgomery would do his best to take them in and care for them.

God has truly blessed me in my business dealings. Some of it is because of Thomas. You remember Thomas, who went to fight in the War between the States. I never told his secret, but he went to fight for the Union. Although I guess you knew that didn't you? You always seemed to know what we were up to, bad or good.

I'm married now to a fine woman, Nancy. We have two sons – Tommy and Nicky. I try to teach them as you taught me and only hope that one day, I can do the hard, difficult task of letting them go.

Danny is doing well too. He was adopted by Josie Evans, a woman I met on the wagon train going out to California. Her son died of cholera, and she asked me if I'd consider letting her adopt him. Danny had always wanted a ma of his own and when I asked him, he agreed. Josie sends him to visit often, and he's grown into a fine young man. His leg never did straighten out as you'd hoped it would, but he's a wonder with animals – horses especially—and soon he'll be buying out a livery business in Coloma, California.

You were right. This was the adventure that I've always wanted to have with my life. Because you told me to leave, I've lived and still live that adventure with my beautiful wife and God by my side.

Thank you, "Papa."

I always wanted to call someone that and tonight I realized, God gave me the best father I could ever have.

Your loving son,

Lee

THE END

Also by Zachary McCrae

Thank you for reading **"The Drifter's Tale"**!

If you liked this book, you can also check out **my full Amazon Book Catalogue at:**
https://go.zacharymccrae.com/bc-authorpage

Thank you!

Made in United States
Troutdale, OR
12/12/2023

15736539R00126